Lies Can Sink Love

James Hanley

A Wings ePress, Inc.
Romance Novel

Wings ePress, Inc.

Edited by: Jeanne Smith
Copy Edited by: Bev Haynes
Executive Editor: Jeanne Smith
Cover Artist: Trisha FitzGerald-Jung
Images: Pixabay

Wings ePress Books
www.wingsepress.com

Copyright © 2024 by: James Hanley
ISBN 979-8-89197-986-4

Published In the United States Of America

Wings ePress, Inc.
3000 N. Rock Road
Newton, KS 67114

Dedication

To all military linguists.

One

Lieutenant Junior Grade Scott Oliver leaned toward the mirror to complete shaving when the shrill doorbell sounded, startling him.

"Shit," he said as blood dripped from a cut on the side of his face. Looking into the hallway, he didn't see either of his roommates going to answer the door, so he did. An attractive young woman, who was behind the door, stiffened and raised her rigid right hand, touching the side of her forehead.

"Permission to come aboard, sir."

Scott returned the salute. "Permission granted."

Julie Bailey entered, moved to Scott, and lifted her head to kiss his cheek. She stopped before reaching his lather-covered face.

"Yuck, Scottie, you're bleeding." Her lips turned down. "Oh no, I bet I did that by pressing the bell while you were shaving.

There's still a dab of cream near your ear." She wet her finger, wiping away the cream. "I can hug you on the other side."

She reached toward him, and he jerked his head, so she pressed against the cut on his cheek. Julie pulled back, "If you got blood in my hair, I'm telling my fiancé. By the way, where is he?"

"Are you looking for me?" Ensign Clayton Taylor came out of the back bedroom barefoot, wearing only his boxers.

Scott said, "Clay, we have a woman in our house; get dressed."

Julie tilted her head, lowering her eyelids. "Look who's talking; you're shirtless. Besides, I've seen Clay in his underwear." Looking at her fiancé, she said, "Don't you dare say it." As soon as she finished speaking, she charged toward Clay, leaped, threw her arms around his neck, and wrapped her legs around his hips.

Staggering from the unexpected embrace, Clay said, "Hey, sweetie, I'm barely awake."

With that, the third roommate, Lieutenant Mark Colburn, came out of his room, rubbing his hand through his hair while suppressing a yawn. "Do you have to make such a racket?" His eyes moved from Clay to Julie. "Oh, it's you two, the almost-married. I usually hear noise *inside* Clay's room, not in the hallway."

When he drew near to the group, Julie slapped Mark's arm.

Mark grabbed the struck bicep. "If you were a sailor, you'd be put in the brig for striking an officer."

She hugged him, "Now I've embraced everyone." Looking at Mark, she said, "I really wish you were coming to our wedding."

"Can't, Jules; I have orders. The guy I'm replacing is leaving Paris early. I'm done with language school with no reason to stall."

"What are you going to do over there?" Julie asked, "Are you spying on the French?"

"No. I'll be the liaison to the French Navy, and I can't tell you anymore unless you have a clearance. Marrying an ensign," he pointed to Clay, "especially that one, doesn't qualify."

"Okay, boys, I'll make breakfast while you all get ready to go to language classes, you to Chinese, Scottie, you to Russian, my love, and to whatever you're doing until you leave, Mark."

After getting dressed, all three went into the small kitchen in their uniforms: a khaki jacket with shoulder boards reflecting their rank, similar-colored pants, and a shirt. All three knotted their dark brown ties as they entered. Julie emptied eggs onto three plates, grabbing strips of sizzling bacon and placing them alongside. Mark, who'd arrived in the room first, volunteered to make the toast while the coffee perked. "You have to pour your own coffee," she instructed them.

Julie sighed. "I'm going to miss Monterey when our time to leave comes. It's so beautiful here, the weather's great, the temperature is near perfect, and there's so much to see."

"Aren't you going to miss Scott and me?" Mark asked.

"Of course." She took a deep breath. "You guys have been my family, but we're all going in different directions; only Clay and I, being the last to report to our duty station, will be here longer than either of you."

"We've all been so busy lately we haven't talked about the house. I'm leaving in a few days, which means a third of the rent is gone," Mark said.

Clay said they couldn't afford to add more to the rent even with two incomes. "Besides, my bride and I would like to be alone; sorry, Scott. We found a new place to live after the honeymoon."

They all stared at Scott.

"I'm looking, but finding an apartment for possibly three or four months at the most is hard. I'll stay here while the honeymooners are away until the end of this month. I hope I'm as lucky as Julie and Clay in finding a new, cheaper place to stay."

The following conversation was largely banter among the Navy men; Julie watched as they went back and forth. She had once said they were like brothers, quick to taunt but willing to support each other if needed; however, the family would soon be separating, as they'd said earlier. She and Clay had promised to contact Mark once they settled into their new place. They all gathered their plates and placed them in the sink.

Mark said, "Thanks for making breakfast, Julie. We'll take care of the plates and utensils later."

She hugged each of them as they gathered at the door, holding their hats in one hand and reaching around Juie in the embrace. Julie held on to Mark the longest, tearing up as she said, "I hope we see you again when we're all overseas if we're assigned to nearby duty stations."

A minute later, Scott came back inside. "What time is the rehearsal dinner on Friday?"

"Why couldn't you ask Clay? You live in the same house."

"I know, he's not good at details. Be at the church by four on Friday; we'll all go to dinner as soon as we finish the rehearsal. Only the bride, groom, best man, maid of honor, and both sets of parents will be there. You'll meet your partner at the church. Denise is a knockout; you'll be the envy of everyone at the wedding."

~ * ~

The three men shared a dinner the night before the rehearsal as a farewell to Mark, who was leaving on Saturday to visit his parents on the East Coast before heading to his duty station in Europe. The packers assigned by the Navy had taken his items, leaving one room in the house vacant. At the same time, Clay boxed some of his possessions, telling Scott that the newly married couple would return to the house after their Hawaii honeymoon to finish moving their belongings to their new rental in Monterey.

"It's smaller, two bedrooms, but one's very small, one bathroom, a small kitchen, and a living room that barely holds the couch Julie is bringing from her apartment, more like a cottage than a house. It's rather plain, but Julie will fix that."

"Wow, the house we've shared is emptying. We've had some great parties there," Mark said.

They toasted the changes in their lives.

~ * ~

The rehearsal dinner was at a local restaurant. As Julie had explained to Scott once, the other members of the wedding group—all friends of the bride and groom—weren't arriving until early Saturday. No other siblings would be there; Julie was an only child, and Clay's brother was on an aircraft carrier in the Mediterranean.

When Scott arrived at the church, he found the two sets of parents with an unfamiliar young woman standing out front chatting. Julie's father said, "The rain is starting, so we should go inside." Before they entered the church's vestibule, Denise Fagella, the maid of honor, greeted Scott, introducing herself. His eyes widened as he looked at her beautiful face. Denise had round, blue eyes highlighted by dark lashes, and her full lips were colored with pink lipstick. Her hair, a deep brown, almost black, was curled at her shoulders. Her curvaceous body was sheathed in a form-fitting dress that stopped above her knees. The future bride and groom were waiting inside. Before he could offer his name, Julie came out.

Julie introduced Scott to Denise by saying, "This is Lieutenant j.g. Scott Oliver."

While still grasping his hand, Denise said, "We met outside. What does j.g. stand for?"

Scott explained that the initials stood for junior grade.

"Does that mean a lesser quality of lieutenant, like grades for honey or syrup?"

Julie screamed, "Denise!"

Scott answered, "Yes, I guess it does. What's your occupation?"

Denise said, "I'm a paralegal."

"Oh," Scott said, "that's like a lawyer j.g."

Denise roared. "Touché." Talking to Julie, she added, grabbing Scott's arm, "I'm going to like this guy."

As they walked into the nave of the church, Scott caught Julie's eyes, his lips forming into a circle as he mouthed the word, *Wow.* Julie chuckled softly. The priest waited at the front of the altar to explain the role of each, with a focus on the bridal couple. Scott and Denise sat in the pew across from the parents. The church still held the odor of incense from an earlier funeral service. The wedding party practiced walking down the aisle and the specifics of the marital ceremony. When the rehearsal was over, the older adults left first; the others followed, chatting while proceeding to the entrance doors. The concrete steps were still wet from the morning rain. Denise reached the edge of the first step, her high heels slipped, and she grabbed Scott's shoulder.

"Hold my hand while we go down the steps," she said.

Even after they reached the sidewalk, she kept her hand in his. Nearing the parked cars, Denise proposed to everyone, "Since Scott and Julie were the drivers, why doesn't Clay ride with her while I ride in Scott's car?"

The restaurant was within ten minutes of the church. On the way, Denise said, "You were introduced to everyone as 'Scott,' but Julie calls you 'Scottie.' Any reason?"

"We have a good relationship, close even though we haven't known each other very long." He tittered as he continued, "They are a great couple but too much alike. Sometimes Julie seeks my advice on dealing with Clay; I go to her when I need a female opinion."

"Is there no other woman in your life you can confide in, no one you're seeing?"

"No to both. I dated someone before I came to Monterey, but the relationship didn't work out. How about you? Are you seeing—"

Denise interrupted Scott by touching his arm while pointing. "There's Julie's folks in front of what must be the restaurant."

Scott parked in a curbside space; Clay and Julie pulled up behind them. The four were met by a maître de at the door. After Julie gave the name of the reservation party, the tuxedoed man led them to the table where the parents had already been seated. After a smiling waitress passed the menus, they all chose their meal, watching the young woman jot down each preference. Most of the conversation was about the wedding, but Julie's father, Warren, looked at Scott when the topic was exhausted.

"Of course, we know what language Clay has been studying and where they're probably going after he's completed the course, but what about you, Scott?" Warren asked.

"I'm in the Chinese language program but haven't received my orders yet, so I don't know my next duty station."

Julie's mother, Magdeline, asked the next question: "How did you get picked for Chinese?"

"I knew the language somewhat. When I was a boy, my parents adopted a timid girl from China. Lilly—that's her name— knew no English. I vowed to help her learn our language, even though I wasn't much older than she and unfamiliar with tonal Chinese. Later, I began studying Mandarin to help her. My high school offered instruction in Asian languages so I could converse with my new sibling while teaching her English. Of course, her school offered special language training. She's fluent now; very much an American young woman."

Julie's mother clapped. "That was very kind. You must be close to your sister."

Scott blushed slightly as the others at the table nodded in agreement. Denise patted his thigh.

"Yes, we're close. I wasn't used to having a sister, only a younger brother. Lilly didn't have siblings in China. Being together suddenly with a girl close to your age was a challenge. But this is a celebration of my two good friends." Standing, he continued: "I know we'll be toasting the couple Sunday, but this is also a good time to offer them best wishes."

The others stood, raising their wine glasses.

When they started to leave, Julie grabbed Scott's arm, pulling him aside.

"Scottie, the parents want a drink at the bar to get to know each other better and discuss the wedding further. Clay and I were asked to join them. It's sort of a family thing. I hope you're not offended."

"No, of course not."

"There's something else; could you drive Denise to her motel?"

"Sure," Scott responded.

"I realize it's a burden to give a ride to a beautiful woman. I'll explain everything to Denise. Thanks so much."

He saw the two women conversing until Denise walked toward him.

"I'm glad you're my chauffeur."

Arriving at the motel, he pulled into a marked space in front of her room.

Denise said, "I'd invite you in, but the place is a mess; my clothes are scattered all over." She moved closer and kissed him, her arms around her neck. The tip of her tongue lightly touched his lips. Pulling back, she started to say something but stopped. Finally, Denise said goodnight, looking at him as she closed the door.

Scott stood in front of the closed door, stunned.

~ * ~

On Saturday, Scott was awakened by the ringing phone. Drowsy after a restless sleep, he walked into the living room and saw Clay talking into the receiver.

"Okay, honey," Clay said, "so today will be busy. Scott just came into the room. Do you want to talk to him?" He handed the phone to Scott. "I'll be right back."

"Hi, Julie."

After a quick greeting, Julie started by explaining the plans for Saturday.

"Whoa," Scott said, "I just woke up. You're talking too fast."

She said, "Okay, I'll go slow. Some of the bridesmaids and one of the groomsmen are flying in this morning, so I'll go with my parents to pick them up; the other groomsmen are local, guys from Clay's class. We have to go to the Hotel Delmonte to check on the room for the reception. After that—"

"Julie, I appreciate you telling me, but why must I know all this?"

"That's true, sorry. I got used to giving you instructions so you can ensure Clay stays with the script. Denise and I will have dinner with the bridesmaids flying in from my hometown and my parents this evening. Denise suggested I invite you."

Scott paused before answering. "Why with your group? I could understand if I was invited to dinner with Clay's family and the other males."

Julie said, "Clay can best explain that part, but his folks are going sightseeing and will dine when they stop touring at whatever time. You know my beloved—not good with schedules. Guess his folks are the same."

"While the thought of being surrounded by you and your bridesmaids is enticing, it's your night with hometown connections. I wouldn't fit in. Count me out."

"I understand." She didn't say a word for seconds. "Scott, how did it go with taking Denise to her motel?"

"Fine; why would you ask that? It was a short drive."

"It's just—never mind. See you at the church." She hung up.

Going back into the room, Clay looked at Scott, who was shaking his head.

Scott said, "Your fiancée can be mysterious."

"I'm marrying her, but it doesn't mean I know what's happening in that pretty head. It'll take me a lot longer, if ever, for that."

~ * ~

Late evening, the phone rang again. Scott picked up; Julie was on the other line.

She explained the logistics for the Sunday wedding and reception. "I know you're driving Clay to the church. Denise and I will arrive by limo. The photographer wants to take outdoor pictures of the bride and groom. I need you to drive Denise to the reception; my folks will drive the bridesmaids; Clay's parents will drive the groomsmen who need a lift. We'll take photos of the wedding party at the hotel before dinner. After the reception, you can take Denise back to her motel. Is that okay?"

"Yes, Captain."

"Very funny. Denise wants to say hello."

After a pause, Denise got on the line. "I'm sorry you couldn't have had a meal with us. You would have been seated with attractive women, although the parents would have monopolized your attention. They asked a lot about you."

"I'm sure I missed a rare opportunity, but I'll see all of you tomorrow to better understand my loss."

"Just don't get any ideas; there will be a lot of beautiful women there, but you're my partner for the evening. I'm looking forward to seeing you, Scottie. I'll put Julie back on."

"Me too, Denise."

"I'm back," Julie said. "Denise is right; you were missed at the dinner."

"I got that sense from Denise. Julie, I know you well enough to detect that you're not telling me something."

"I'm just a bit uptight, wedding jitters, I guess."

On Sunday morning, Scott was putting on his dress-white uniform, attaching the shoulder boards while Clay was doing the same in his room. They met in the living room, inspecting each other, and drove in Scott's car to Saint Peter's Church in Pacific Grove, parking in the church lot. They stood in the narthex until the other groomsmen arrived. Scott and Clay took their places at the side of the altar, waiting for the bride to proceed down the carpeted nave. Guests arrived, taking a seat in pews on either side. The organist played when the priest stepped out from behind the altar, nodding at the two Naval officers. Denise and the other bridesmaids entered, and the conversations among the guests stopped suddenly when Julie followed, holding her father's arm.

Scott said softly, "She's gorgeous."

Clay looked at Scott and back toward the women. "Are you talking about Julie or Denise?"

Scott didn't answer. Julie kissed her father and moved beside Clay. After exchanging the vows, the newly married left the church, walking under a bridge of crossed swords. Rice coated the concrete steps to the limo parked at the curb. The remaining guests poured out and headed to their vehicles. Denise touched Scott's arm.

"I gather you have your instructions; you're my driver again," she said.

"Best looking passenger ever in my car. You are beautiful."

Denise squeezed his arm. "You look great in your uniform, all white and virginal."

Scott chuckled. "I've never been called that. The Navy doesn't use that term to describe the uniform."

The reception was held at the Naval Postgraduate School in the Delmonte Hotel. The outside front area consisted of a circle of national flags surrounding a round pool edged with trimmed bushes. The main entrance was through the Peacock Lawn, a garden of rose plantings, boxwood hedges, and gravel paths. Inside the building, round-back chairs were placed about; two side windows looked out on a cactus garden; stones bordered separated sections of plants and trees. The large rectangular ballroom had a high, sculptured ceiling with iron chandeliers. An ornate tiled fountain dominated a corner of the room. Circular, white-clothed tables festooned with a tower of pale flowers at the bridal table filled the space inside, leaving a section for later dancing.

When the guests arrived, the wedding party made their entrance with background music from a small band. After the crowd had settled, Scott gave his best man speech, followed by raised glasses at the tables. The guests got up to dance between the servings, and Denise pulled Scott toward the floor, pressing close to him while they moved in slow circles. Denise took the chair when one of the men in the groom's party seated next to Scott left to sit with his wife at another table. They talked between dances. Each time the music slowed, she reached for him. The bride and groom stayed seated, watching the movement on the dance floor, especially the best man and his date. Scott noticed the newlyweds were staring at him and Denise; they whispered to each other after each glance.

The reception ended while the sky was still light, but the nighttime darkness was approaching. Scott and Denise walked to his car. Before she got in, she asked, "Can we stop by the beach? Living in Indiana, I don't get to see the ocean."

Scott drove to the parking area at Carmel Beach. Before she got out of the car, Denise lifted her dress and rolled down her unclipped stockings. Scott turned the other way until she released her stockings. Standing barefoot in front of him, she looked down disapprovingly at his feet. Scott removed his shoes, and they walked onto the sand. After a few steps, she took his hand as they walked to the ocean's edge. The waves slapped the shore, tossing a mist of salt water that clung to their clothes. The moon was in full phase, lighting the top of the foamy waves. The wind came off the water, lifting her hair. She walked into the retreating water after the waves broke while looking toward him. As he stood by her, she put her arm around his waist; he reciprocated. They stood there saying nothing, the sole figures on the empty beach. She reached across and touched his face with her free hand while sliding her arm from his back. When Scott looked toward her, her face was close to his. They moved toward each other until they were kissing. An unexpected wave stopped them, dampening their clothes, but their embrace never loosened. She leaned close to his ear, "I want us to make love." Her breathing quickened as she looked into his eyes for a response. Instead of answering, Scott led her back to the car, neither of them putting on their shoes.

At her motel, she fumbled for the key. Once finding it, she circled the lock until Scott gently took the key from her hand to open the door. Inside, she looked at him. "I had to ask the maid to help me zip up."

Scott pulled at the zipper of the high-collared gown, slowly lowering it until the top of her shoulders appeared. Kissing her neck, he unzipped further, freed the dress, and, placing his hands on her waist, gradually slipped the garment down until it fell to her feet. In a rapid motion, she kicked the dress free. "My turn," she whispered while unbuttoning his jacket. As if in agreed sequence, he removed her slip, leaving her in her underwear. They stopped undressing to kiss. Her tongue reached inside his mouth. The urgency increased, and both were soon naked, still standing. Scott yanked the covers from the bed, his breath stopping momentarily as he stared at her nudity. Sitting at the edge of the bed, he touched her gently, and she tossed her head back. Denise put her hands on his chest, pushing him backward until he was flat on the bed. Lying together, they made love.

Both were panting when they stared at the ceiling. Scott lifted to his elbows to open his mouth to speak when she put her finger over his lips. "Don't say anything; let's savor the next few minutes."

They fell asleep until morning. She woke first and took a bathrobe from her suitcase.

Leaning over Scott, she said, "Get up. I need to get ready for my flight."

"Hmm," he muttered. Lifting slightly from the bed, his eyes puffy, he yawned. "What time is it?"

"It's six. "

Scott groaned. "Come back to bed."

"Scottie, I can't. You have a class today, don't you? I have too much to do before going to the airport. I don't want to miss my flight."

"I'll teach you Chinese obscenities if we stay," he said, his head tilted.

She tugged at his arm, which was hanging off the bed. "Get up, Scottie."

He lifted the sheet, his only covering; peering under, he said, "I'm up; wanna see?"

"I'll lie beside you for two minutes without peeking under the sheet or anything else."

They stayed in an embrace until she said, "Okay. That's enough. Now get moving, sailor. You have to go home, get cleaned up, go to class."

"But I need to drive you to the airport."

She leaned over to kiss him. "I'll get a cab. I don't want you to get in trouble because of me. I'm going to take a shower..." When she saw the look in his eyes, she said, "Alone! I'll be getting ready for a while, so we should say goodbye now. I'm so glad I met you, especially glad we had this time together. I'll remember this for a very long time."

"Wait a minute. You're talking as if we won't see each other again."

"Scott, I live in Indiana, and you're here. I've applied for law school in my state and have a job. You're going overseas in about four months, as you told me. I regret leaving you now; how difficult would it be when *you* go away if we continue? I care about you. Our lives are too complicated, too separate."

"So, this was a classical one-night stand?"

Her voice was strained. "I will cherish this time we spent together; don't cheapen it with a cliché. We don't have time to discuss this."

"I want to see you again. We have to work out the logistics, but I agree we don't have enough time to do that now."

"I'll leave my phone number, and you jot down yours. We'll talk." She took the pen and the pad on the small desk to write her phone number. Putting her hand on his cheek, she kissed him.

~ * ~

Back at the house, Scott was taken aback by the quiet. Three men and a frequent female visitor—Julie—had kept the place lively; now, he was alone. In addition, he'd slept with a woman who intrigued him. A few days later, he called Denise.

"Hi," he said, "it's good to hear your voice. I've missed seeing you."

"I miss you, too, Scott. We had a good time together, didn't we?"

"I thought it was more than that; I hope I get a chance to meet with you again."

"How's school? I hope I didn't distract you when we were together."

"Classes are fine. If you'd be around, I could take a few days off to travel to your location."

"Now's not a good time; my schedule is pretty full, even today, meaning I can't stay on the line long."

"Okay," Scott said, "I won't keep you. Why don't you call me some night when you're free; we can talk more then."

"Will do; have a good day," Denise said.

A week later, Scott called Denise again and got her answering machine. She did call him back, but their conversation was short, cordial, and emotionless. Scott asked about arranging to see each other, but again, she was non-committal.

He received a call from Julie inviting him to their new house. Scott arrived carrying a bottle of wine. The furnished house was small but attractive in Monterey's crowded but well-maintained neighborhood. The ocean theme was apparent in the wall colors, the seaside paintings on the walls, the soft blue color of the cushioned chairs, and sea shells as trays. According to Julie in their last phone conversation, the kitchen had been recently updated with new appliances; a skylight drew in the remnants of the setting sun. Julie hugged Scott; Clay came in from the deck to greet his prior roommate.

"Clay is cooking steaks on the grill; they'll be done shortly," Julie said. "It's a beautiful evening, so let's all go outside.

They went onto the deck and sat on the folding chairs; Clay jumped up periodically to check on the meat.

"How was the honeymoon?" Scott asked.

"Hawaii was wonderful," Julie said. "The weather was great; as you can see from our fading tans, we spent a lot of time on the beach. Clay talked me into parasailing, but I was frightened the whole time."

Clay joked, "So much so, she went up twice more before we left."

"I heard from Denise when we got back. She said the two of you had a strong connection, even have spoken a few times since the wedding," Julie said.

"Connection is a good word. We discussed working out the logistics so I could see her again. However, I knew things were different, that she was backing away, not only because of the phone conversation but what she called me. This may sound like an odd reason; at first, she called me Scottie, copying you," he said, looking at Julie.

"I noticed what she called you, beginning the night before the wedding," Julie said.

"Yes, but before she left the motel to go to the airport, she called me 'Scott' as well as in the phone calls."

Julie leaned forward, her voice rising, "Wait a minute, did you spend the night with her? Denise told me she got a cab to the airport."

Clay chuckled. "Julie, I guess we weren't the only one having..." Julie's stabbing glare stopped him.

"She never mentioned your tryst." Julie was breathing heavily through her nose.

"I wouldn't call it a *tryst*."

"Scottie, stop stalling! Did you have sex with my maid of honor?"

"Yes. I love you, Julie, but Denise and I are adults, capable of making life decisions. Clearly, from the communication since then, nothing else will happen. I've wondered if I said or did something wrong. On the phone calls, I felt I was talking to someone different, someone cold."

"Do you want to know why? I'll tell you; it's..." Her voice was rising.

Clay cut her off. "That's enough, Julie. You're too angry to explain. Scott, Denise is engaged; obviously, she didn't share that with you."

Scott sat back stiffly, his eyes going back and forth between his friends.

Julie got up from her chair and walked to him. Putting her arms around his shoulders, her eyes were moist. She said, "I'm sorry, Scottie. I'm really mad at Denise. She shouldn't have deceived you. I know you well enough that you wouldn't have gotten involved with her if you'd known. I'm also mad at myself. We saw you two were getting close at the wedding, but I said nothing to you then."

Scott patted Julie's arm. "Okay, but it shouldn't ruin your friendship with her. We all need to move on. That Sunday was your wedding; don't let what happened between Denise and me cloud your memories of that day. Besides, *she* should have told me she was engaged. You're right; I wouldn't have gotten involved with her if I'd known."

Julie was back in her seat. "Denise is my best friend but can be flirtatious, but never more than that. She cared for you,

Scottie, I'm certain. I don't know what's going through her mind now. I don't plan to mention what happened between the two of you when I next speak to her, although it will be difficult not to yell at her." She said to Clay, "Didn't we get an expensive bottle of Scotch from your uncle? Now might be the best time to open it."

While they sipped the scotch, Julie and Clay talked mostly about their Hawaii honeymoon, Clay keeping an eye on the cooking steaks until they were ready. Julie asked Scott to help her set the table inside as Clay flipped the meat onto a large plate. Gathering utensils from the kitchen drawer, Scott felt Julie's hand on his arm.

"You're disappointed about Denise, aren't you?"

"Yes, there were obvious obstacles for us to continue any relationship, but I was willing to try."

"Just don't feel you did something wrong."

Hearing Clay near the table, Scott and Julie entered the dining room with the plates and utensils. Before sitting, Scott opened the wine.

Clay said, "We'll be over tomorrow to get the few things at the house. You only have a few days left before you have to leave. Where are you going to live?"

Putting down his fork, Scott explained, "I've had a hard time finding a place. New classes are starting at language school; arrivals at the Naval Postgraduate School and language school are scooping up the local rentals. Any apartment owner would prefer someone who can sign a lease for longer than I can; a house by myself is too costly for a junior officer. I found an apartment complex on Cypress Avenue in Pacific Grove willing to offer a short-term rental. I'm meeting with the landlord tomorrow to discuss the arrangement."

Clay dropped his knife, and the blade struck against the plate. "Scott, I have guys in my class who live there. They are all married, and all are enlisteds. From what I've heard, no officers live in that complex. A few residents are civilians, but most in those apartments are military, attending language courses. Won't you feel awkward?"

"Why should that matter? An officer can't live in a development with enlisteds?"

Clay answered, "Oh, my sweet, you will better understand when we go to our first duty station. Officers and enlisted can work together, be cordial, and respect each other, but their personal lives can't mix. Fraternization is discouraged in the military, based on the belief that friendship between officers and enlisted can undermine authority and discipline."

Julie's response was blatantly sarcastic. "You sound like you're quoting from a manual."

Scott added to Clay's comments, "Julie, Clay is right. On most installations, you'll find an officers' club and an enlisted club for dinners and events. Base housing will also be divided. You will meet other wives who will befriend you, but they will be married to officers. It's just how it is, whether or not we agree with it."

"But I'm not an officer," she protested, "why can't I have friends married to enlisted men?"

Clay interjected. "Enlisted wives are also discouraged from friendship with officers' wives. If an officer dates an enlisted woman, especially one reporting to him, his career could be over."

"Does that mean if I see the wife of an enlisted sailor, I should avoid her?"

"No, my dear spouse, you don't have to run from her."

Scott could see she had a devious expression on her face. "If her husband is in the Army or Air Force, do I have to snub her?"

"Doesn't matter which service, because the rules are all the same," Scott said.

"Bunch of silly rules," Julie huffed.

Scott and Clay looked at each other.

"Back to my original question before we were interrupted by my radical wife, how do you feel about being the only officer in an apartment complex where the other residents are enlisted?"

"I don't know. Perhaps I can live there without making my rank known. Considering the lack of available short-term rentals, I don't have a choice."

Julie interjected. "That's what I don't get. Okay, I'll reluctantly concede that officers and enlisted can't mix, yada yada yada while on base or a ship, but you will be living in apartments that are not on a military installation. Again, why should rank make a difference there?"

"Honey, it's more than a set of rules; it's a mindset that carries off base," Clay answered.

"I give up," she said.

They finished the evening with coffee and dessert. Before saying goodbye, Scott said, "I'll give you my phone number after I settle in the apartment, but please don't give the number to Denise."

Julie called Scott a day later. "I know what you told us, but I heard from Denise, and she is very apologetic and wanted your phone number so she could explain."

"Did you offer to give it to her?" Scott asked.

"No, I told her you were moving but was honest with her that I would not be providing your number because you asked me not to. She's upset with me. There were so many things I wanted to say to her, like why did she seduce you yet not tell you she was planning to get married."

"She didn't *seduce* me; I was very willing to get physical. What's the sense of talking to her? I don't need an apology if that's the reason; what would we say further? Do I wish her congratulations?"

"Okay," Julie sighed.

"You don't agree, do you?"

"Scottie, it's not my call. She's a nice person who made a mistake, admittedly at your expense. I don't see the harm in hearing her out."

"Why are you pushing this? If I talk to her, where would it lead? Are you choosing sides?"

"I'm not choosing sides; you know how fond I am of you. But I believe she really cares for you. Maybe it would be to appease her conscience or to apologize. I do believe the time with you was not an insignificant event for her. She could be questioning the engagement."

"How can you know all that? Did she say something to you after the wedding or on the phone?"

"She didn't have to. I could see it in her eyes when she looked at you at the rehearsal dinner and the wedding. One time before the ceremony, I asked her what she thought of you, and her face lit up. She said you were 'nice,' but her expression told me a lot more. When I was growing up, I spent time with my grandmother. She taught me that you could learn more from a person's face than their words. Once, she invited me to watch when she had her friends over for tea. I watched their faces, and she was right. Their expressions were as revealing as the words they spoke. My grandmother knew when they were bluffing or had a good hand. When they complimented someone, Gran could tell when they were insincere. I learned a lot that day. Helps when I play strip poker with Clay," she added. "I can't say she was falling for you, but I believe she wasn't far from it."

"If she doubts getting married, she must resolve that alone. Tell her again *I* don't want the number revealed when I get it, and that will get you off the hook."

They talked for a few minutes more before hanging up.

~ * ~

On Saturday, Scott drove to the apartment complex on Cypress Avenue, just south of a major east-west road. The front entrance was a square with a black lentil and brick steps leading to the lower level. Wrought-iron steps at each corner of the complex led to the second-level units. Parking spaces were on each side of the building, except for the front. Walking inside, he looked at the large pool rimmed by blue-colored concrete; the chlorinated water was an aqua color. A few folding webbed chairs were scattered around the pool's edge; a ladder was at the far end of the deeper water. Before arriving, Scott had called the building manager, who'd explained that she lived in the first apartment off the entrance to the left. He knocked on the door of apartment 101, and a small woman opened it. She introduced herself as Mrs. Redman.

"My husband and I manage the building, handling any apartment problems. My Ron is very handy, and we have contacts if he can't fix it."

"Mrs. Redman, I explained that I'm taking a class at the language school and need a place for three months, four at the most until I report to a duty station. I know I may be the only officer in the complex and..."

"You would be. There are forty-eight apartments, mostly occupied by young men also taking language courses, all living here with their wives. Word-of-mouth referrals keep a constant flow of students. Six apartments are occupied by tenants not in the military, including Arthur Willis, who lives next to your place. Arthur is an older man retiring soon; his family has gone to their new residence in Virginia until he joins them in a few months. No children are allowed here. The pool is too great a liability with kids around."

"I started to explain that enlisted personnel are uncomfortable around officers in a social setting. I think it's best that no one here knows my rank so I can talk to residents without awkwardness."

"I know about the military's notion of fraternizing—can't say I agree with it—but it'll be a challenge to hide your rank coming in and out. As you know, Naval officers' and enlisteds' uniforms are very different. Luckily, the available apartment is across from here and is also the end unit with a parking lot in the back of the building. You can enter and leave through the small passageway in the shadow of the upstairs apartments into the parking area outside. There's always a risk you'll be seen, but it's the best spot to avoid detection if that's what you want. The folks living here are very social; if you avoid contact, you will stick out, leading to curiosity. Sometimes, this place reminds me of a small town where rumors and gossip are rampant."

"Thanks for your thoughts. I'll leave early; at the end of the day, I go to the gym near the school, bringing civilian clothes to change into before coming back here. If I'm discovered, so be it."

Mrs. Redman led Scott to the apartment he would rent. The rooms were all of a single color, and the furnishings were nondescript and worn. Two bedrooms flanked the bathroom. The galley kitchen contained wood cabinets, a pitted sink, and chrome-edged appliances. A wooden table with three chairs made up the eating area. A large window filled the upper portion of the wall above the table.

"Pot, pans, and utensils are in the kitchen drawers. We provided a few, but people who stayed previously added a few items, giving you much to select from as needed."

"I'm not a cook, so the kitchen has all I'll need. I will eat out a lot or order in."

"I'm sure you saw the pool area when you came in, but you may want to look longer."

They stepped outside onto the concrete front. Scott looked at the pool, which took up most of the courtyard.

"The pool seemed inviting when I came, and I plan to use it."

Mrs. Redman said, "Residents love the pool. We take good care of it. A man comes weekly to clean the water and check the chlorine level. I hope you'll be staying here for a while. The furnished apartments have been called 'functional,' not meant as a compliment. There is a constant turnover, especially for the language students who stay about a year, so it's adequate for them. It's one of the least expensive places to stay around here, which is good for the military men."

"The apartment will suit me fine."

"Having mostly young people here makes for a lively complex: parties around the pool, music playing during birthday celebrations and departures, all with plenty of food. Being military, the folks here are respectful of others, no late parties outside, and after any event, folks clean up. I know you want to keep your rank hidden, but I hope doing so doesn't keep you from enjoying the activities."

"Mrs. Redman, you've sold me on the apartment. I'd like to move in on Monday after class. I don't have much, mostly clothes."

They shook hands, and as they started to leave, a man came out of the apartment next door.

"Oh, Arthur, I want you to meet your neighbor, Scott Oliver. Scott, this is Arthur Willis."

Willis was a tall man with gray hair mixed with a few strands of dark brown. His face was lined, and his pants hung below his stomach. He shook Scott's extended hand with the vigor of priming a pump.

"Most residents call me *Pop* to tease, but they invite me to all their shindigs." He looked at Mrs. Redman. "Am I showing my age? Do they still use that word?"

"It's good to meet you, Arthur. I won't call Pop," Scott said.

"I don't know if our delightful landlady told you, but I'm only here for a few months before retiring. My family is settling into our new house. I can't wait to join them."

Scott explained, "I won't be here much longer than you. I'll be finishing my studies and getting my orders."

"I was in the Coast Guard, so I'm familiar with how things work in the military, even though I served long ago. You'll fit in well with the young crowd here, but if you need anything, have any questions, or want to know the latest apartment gossip, feel free to knock on my door."

~ * ~

Scott's class ended early on Monday. Changing out of his uniform, he drove from the rented house to the apartment complex. He stopped by Mrs. Redman to get the key and, after sharing a cup of coffee, walked to his place, dropping his possessions in the spare bedroom. The weather was warmer than typical for the time of year, and he stepped outside to look around, leaning on the railing outside his door. Responding to a few women waving in greeting, he stared at the pool, blue-green from the sun beating on the still water. Scott went back inside, changed into a bathing suit, and walked to the pool with a towel over his shoulders. Diving in the closest end, he surfaced and swung his arms into a rhythmic motion, glancing sideways with each stroke, the chlorinated water blurring his vision as he swam to the other end of the pool. He was in his tenth lap when he saw shapely legs in the water near the far edge. Stopping his strokes, he trod water while looking toward the source of the feet in the pool. He shook his head to clear his vision and saw a beautiful young woman, her hair pulled back in a ponytail, her wide eyes staring at him. She wore an open cotton cover over a one-piece bathing suit.

"Am I keeping you from swimming?"

"No, you're not. Just came out to soak my legs." Before Scott could say anything further, she stood, nodded, and walked back to the apartment door near where she sat.

Scott shrugged and said to himself, "Then why wear a bathing suit?" and began his lap across the pool, lifting his head a bit higher when he neared where she had been seated.

He saw the young woman from the pool again in an animated conversation with another woman, both leaning in as if sharing words they didn't want overheard. While the distance was too great to determine a relationship between the two, he suspected they were sisters by some common features and similar walk as they circled the pool. Both wore skirts that ended above their knees and a short-sleeved blouse. His eyes were drawn mainly to the one he'd seen with her legs in the water. For a moment, she looked in his direction. He thought he saw a brief smile on her face, but she quickly turned away. Entering an apartment together, they increased his suspicion about their relationship; just as the door closed, she looked at him with an expression of unmistakable recognition.

~ * ~

Scott had finished showering the following weekend when the phone rang; it was Clay.

"Julie's shopping with some friends and I'd like to see your new place. Are you good for today?"

"Sure, I had nothing planned that can't wait; was just going to do laundry."

A few hours later, Clay knocked on Scott's door. Entering the apartment, he looked around.

"You've done a lot with the place," he said facetiously.

"I'm only here for a few months, so what's the purpose of adding to the furniture."

"You were that way at the house, never adding pictures or knickknacks. We joked that your room was like a monk's cell. I'll send my interior decorator; she'll suggest making this apartment look more lived-in."

"You're talking about your wife. Julie does have good taste, except in her choice of spouse."

"Let's go outside; I'm really impressed with the pool, which takes up most of the courtyard," Clay said.

They stood in front, looking toward the colorful water. A couple came out of the apartment in the other section and waved. Scott waved back.

"People seem pretty friendly. Has your secret slipped—that you are an officer?"

"No," Scott answered, pointing to the exit on the other side of his apartment. "I can sneak out early in the morning and change into civvies at the gym before coming back here. I'm not being overly secretive, but you know why. I plan to keep my secret for as long as I can. People are friendly, at least as I've experienced in a short time, but could that be different if they knew I was an officer?"

"Julie met a few of the wives of enlisted in my class when she drove me for a few days while my car was being repaired. I got a long complaint on the topic of separation in the Navy. She will struggle when we get to our duty station where the rule is enforced even stronger."

"If people learn about my rank, I can live with it. I'm not here long."

"Have you met anyone yet, talked to them?"

"Not yet, just to say hello or to wave, as you saw. Actually, I met my neighbor, an older man who is staying in the apartments until he retires soon." Scott paused. "I did sort of meet a pretty young woman. I was swimming in the pool and looked up to see her sitting on the edge with her feet in the water. I asked if she was coming in, but she declined, walking away. I saw her once after that. She was with another woman, I think was her sister. I swear she noticed me looking at her, especially when she glanced toward this way before going into her apartment."

"What you're saying is that you haven't really met her. You probably don't know her name; if so, she knows nothing about you. How can you find out who she is; most importantly, is she married?"

Scott said, "I know. My next-door neighbor, Arthur, offered to share the gossip about the apartments. He'd probably know who she is. According to the landlord, most everyone is with a spouse taking language courses, so one of the two could be a friend from the development or visiting from somewhere else, but I think they're related. Unless two siblings are married to sailors attending language school, which is highly unlikely, one could be unmarried and a guest."

"Okay, Sherlock; instead of speculating," Clay said, "Let's ask your neighbor. Since no one is on the right side of your place, it has to be this one on the left."

Before Scott could discourage him, Clay knocked on the door. When Arthur opened the door, he looked puzzled to see Clay on the other side but recognized Scott.

"I'll come out," he said, "the place is a mess. What can I do for you boys?"

"My friend, Scott, briefly met an attractive young woman who lives—" Clay paused, looking at Scott. "By the way, my name is Clay."

"While swimming, I saw her go back into apartment nineteen," Scott provided. "She's young..."

"Very attractive, too, apparently," Clay added.

"I bet that's Melinda. You have a good eye, Scott; she's the only single woman in the complex. Striking, too. The apartment is rented by her sister, Diane, who is here with her Navy husband, Luke. Melinda is here for a brief time, as she explained when Diane introduced me one day, but it seems like more than a few days, perhaps even a few weeks, so far."

"There are no other single women except for her?" Clay asked. "Not that I'm interested; I'm married," he quickly added.

"The majority of the occupants are military attending language school. A few couples are not attached to the service, but they are all young, except for me and a middle-aged man who lives quietly on the second level toward the back. In fact, only one woman wears the uniform; she and her husband are assigned to the language school. All the other women are here with their enlisted husbands. It's 1983—maybe the number of women taking language courses will change in time. We also have a couple, Jeff and Debbie, who are," he lowered his voice, "Hippies. You can smell the pot if you walk by their apartment when their windows are open." He guffawed.

"How do you know so much about the residents here?" Scott asked.

"Pity! I'm an old man here by himself with marginal cooking aptitude and equally incompetent household skills. Some of the women, including Diane and Melinda, drop off food. I often get invited to dinner. Sometimes, I get a knock on the door, and someone will say they're going to the store asking if I need anything. I'm always invited to the parties around the pool. They are a great group of people. I admit," he said, smiling, "I milk the situation a bit."

"How come you're here; you don't fit the profile of a renter, as Scott described. He mentioned you were retiring. Where do you work?" Clay asked.

"As I explained to Scott, I'm here temporarily to finish my job at the *San Francisco Chronicle* before retiring. I cover the area south of the city, which includes Monterey. A lot goes on down here: the growth of high-tech, emerging wineries, tourism, of course, the golf tournament. I hope you enjoy your stay, and I am glad to meet you, Clay."

"Does he know you're an officer?" Clay asked after Arthur went into his apartment.

"No, but if anyone can figure it out, I bet he can."

In Scott's apartment, they drank beer at the small table.

"Has Julie heard from Denise again?" Scott asked.

"Yes, my wife has forgiven her best friend but is still irritated by how Denise deceived you. They don't talk about the lie to avoid a disagreement. Julie has not given her your phone number as she promised. By the way, you'll be invited to dinner again soon. Julie wants to finish getting the place settled."

"Your house looked pretty complete to me," Scott said.

"You know how she is, always fussing, always improving. That's one of the reasons I love her."

~ * ~

Scott found that the weather helped his stealth. Fog often rolled in during summer, providing a gray mist that limited visibility. Slipping out the door and hurrying around the corner to his car in the back lot during the morning was easy, allowing him to avoid encountering any residents. There were a few close calls, but his movements were so quick that anyone in sight might not have noticed when he left in uniform. As planned, he changed at the gym, which was a wise choice, he realized, since apartment dwellers were outside later in the day.

Late on a weekday, Scott stepped outside and heard a shriek. Looking toward the far end of the first level, he saw a woman dressed in a two-piece bathing suit run toward the pool and jump into the water. The splash hid her from view, but once she lifted her head above the water, Scott thought she was the same young woman who had sat on the edge when he was swimming.

She was still in the pool when Scott approached. Melinda wiped the drops from her eyes to look up at him.

"So that's why you wanted the pool to yourself last time. That's quite an entrance."

"That's very funny. Help me out." She lifted her hand toward him, and Scott grabbed on, pulling her to the side of the pool. Not letting go, he looked at Melinda.

She blushed and looked down at her fingers. "I'm out now."

"Sorry," Scott said as he released. "I'm Scott Oliver; I live at the end unit."

"You are the mysterious tenant. There's been a lot of curiosity and speculation about you. There aren't too many single occupants here." She glanced down at his left hand as she spoke. "I guess you're in the bachelor section, along with Arthur."

"Except Arthur is not single." He looked at her eyes, slightly red from the chlorine, but the chemical didn't diminish the green irises. Her mouth was sensuous, with pouting lips and an easy smile. She pushed back the wet hair that hung down her back to just below her shoulders. She said something, but not concentrating on her words, he asked her to repeat.

"My name is Melinda Jenkins. I'm living temporarily with my older sister, who's married to a petty officer attending language school."

"Temporarily?"

Before Melinda could respond, another woman came out of the apartment.

"Speaking of my sister, here she comes. Diane, this guy at the end apartment has two first names."

"Scott Oliver," he said, extending his hand.

"I'm glad to meet you, Scott. I see you met my kid sister."

"Yes, we just met, although she snubbed me once before."

The door to their apartment opened and a handsome man approached the three, putting his arm around Diane.

"Scott Oliver, this is my husband, Petty—"

He interrupted her and offered his hand to Scott. "Luke Durham. There are some rules in this complex. We don't talk about our ratings, or anything related to the military, except we may mention the language we're learning or how long before we ship out. We're civilians while we're here."

Scott puffed his breath in relief. "Is that the only rule?" he asked.

"One or two more," Luke said. "Anytime there is a party, you must bring beer to the festivities. As you can imagine, these apartments aren't large enough for a crowd to gather inside. So we get together mostly around the pool. You'll meet many of the other apartment dwellers at those times."

Luke looked at her sister-in-law. "Melinda, you have goosebumps and you're shaking slightly. Are you cold?"

"Yes," she answered, as the sun had slipped behind the clouds. I'm going in. Goodbye, Scott Oliver. Hope to see you again."

After they left, Scott jumped in the pool and swam from one end to the other. On his fifth lap, he paused, looking toward where Melinda was living. He thought he saw someone peering below a raised blind. Grabbing the towel he'd placed on a webbed chair, he walked back toward his apartment, his mind on the young woman he saw jumping in the water. She remained on his mind as he cooked a hamburger on the gas range. Scott realized that the meeting with her, Diane, and Luke was his first interaction with other residents, except for Arthur. He was encouraged by the apartments' rule that would allow him to avoid revealing that he was an officer. He knew he also had additional motivation to continue the deception—thanks to the rule. Melinda wasn't military, and he wondered if she understood the fraternization rules. Still, she would likely be influenced by her brother-in-law as well as the other enlisted in the apartment complex.

~ * ~

Scott was sitting on the couch studying his language material when he heard voices and a knock on the door next to his. One voice he heard was Arthur's before the door closed. About fifteen minutes later, someone was at *his* door. When he opened it, he was greeted by three women, one holding a plastic tray with something wrapped in aluminum foil in the center. He recognized Diane and Melinda.

"We know you single guys don't get a home-cooked meal often, so we want to offer you one," Diane said.

Scott was looking at Melinda, and she was returning his gaze.

"Scott Oliver, this is Mariam Longstern. She was the chef while I helped. Melinda made the dessert."

Mariam, a pleasant-faced, short woman, stepped forward to shake his hand. Scott invited them in, but as the last woman entered, he panicked.

"Excuse me a moment. I want to shut the door to my bedroom; it's a mess."

Mariam said, "We're married, except for Melinda; we're used to messy men."

"I'll be just a minute—could you place the food on the kitchen counter?" Once in the bedroom, he glanced at his uniform spread out on his bed and quickly shut the door. He encouraged the three to stay in the living room for a while. Grabbing a chair from the dining room table, he sat while the women settled on the couch.

"How often do you feed us poor, single orphans?" Scott teased.

"We don't take special orders, if that's what you're asking. But you won't starve to death," Mariam said, smiling.

"I'm looking forward to the meal and appreciate you taking the time to make extra for me. I gather Arthur is also a recipient. I was going to leave for takeout; I'm glad I didn't miss you."

"Just heat it in the oven for about fifteen minutes; the smaller item is a slice of homemade cake Melinda made."

Looking at Melinda, he grinned, "Are you a baker by trade?"

"No, hardly an amateur."

"I think I'll swim after eating to help digest the great food. Will you be in the pool later, Melinda?"

She blushed. "Not today, but definitely late afternoon tomorrow."

Mariam said, "We'll leave you with the food; must feed our spouses."

The women left after a short time. With the door open, Scott saw Diane put her arm around her sister and heard her say, "He was pretty obvious, wasn't he?"

Melinda chuckled. "There is an advantage to being the only single girl around here."

After heating the dinner, he ate at the kitchen table.

~ * ~

The next day, when Scott came out of his apartment in his trunks and a towel around his shoulders, he saw Melinda was already in the water at the shallow end near her sister's apartment. He walked over and stepped into the pool. Even though the late-day sun was weak, the air temperature was mild; he shivered slightly entering the water, "It's still a bit cold," he said.

"I know," Melinda responded. "I'm getting out."

She dog-paddled to the edge. Scott followed behind her. Once on the concrete, he dried his chest with his towel. Melinda watched his movements.

"I forgot to bring a towel, so I'll go inside."

"Don't," Scott said, a bit louder than he'd intended. "You can use mine; I'll sun dry."

"There's not a lot of sun," she said.

He put the towel around her shoulders, patting the terrycloth to blot the drops on her back. Melinda took the ends of the towel from his hands, her fingers lingering on his hands. He walked to the nearby chairs, dragging a straight-back chair and a folding one. Melinda took the reclining chair; she lay on the webbing, soon closing her eyes.

"I love this time," she said, "when it's not full day and not quite night."

Scott tried not to look at her body stretched across the chair but failed until she sat up, raising the chair back upright.

"What made you join the Navy?"

"After graduating college, I had no idea what I wanted to do with my life, so I thought maybe the military would provide training to give me direction. I also wanted to travel, thinking the Navy is the best source of free exploration."

She looked at him quizzically. "As a college graduate, why didn't you apply to become an officer?"

Scott swallowed before answering. "There are a lot of college grads who are enlisted."

"If you say so. Luke hopes he'll be stationed in one place so he can take courses, but that's not the same as you."

"I recall I asked you why you came here, but we were interrupted before you could answer. I know you've been here for a while."

"How do you know?" She paused her sentence; "You've been talking to Arthur. He's a dear man but a gossip. Guess that comes with being a reporter."

"Don't deflect."

Melinda continued. "I got my degree from a local college and got an entry-level job in human resources at a distribution center in the next town. In high school, I dated a boy, and our relationship was put on hold because he attended an out-of-state university while I went to a local college. We reconnected after graduation. We had plans," Melinda paused, "but then we broke up."

"You quit your job and came to Pacific Grove because the relationship ended?"

"Not right away. I stayed home for a while, but there were too many memories. I'd been working for about a year for a wonderful boss. She said I could take a leave of absence of up to two months, and she knew someone who could fill in. I don't think I'll need all that time."

"Do you know when you'll go back?"

"No. My sister and brother-in-law have been very supportive, and being far from home has been helpful. I don't know the timing."

"I'm glad you came to Pacific Grove," he said.

"Scott, some people are already trying to match us, particularly Mariam, after your question about meeting at the pool. I'm not ready for a relationship right now, and I've told Mariam that."

"I don't want to date someone now either. I'm only here for a few months until I get orders, so getting involved has no purpose. You're very easy to talk to. Most people wouldn't be comfortable sharing personal details so soon after meeting."

Melinda leaned over and offered her hand. "I had the same thought about you. We agree on dating, but we can be unattached friends."

"Are you coming to the party next Saturday?" she asked.

"I wasn't aware there would be one. I didn't get invited."

"You don't need an invitation. Since you're not much of a cook, you can bring refreshments; unlike what my brother-in-law says, it doesn't have to be beer. Two women in this complex are pregnant, and some of us don't like the taste. I'm going in now. I hope to see you at the outdoor festivities, friend."

As she walked toward her apartment, Scott called out, "You still have my towel."

"I know," she said. "I'll give it back washed and folded. I bet you're not good at that either."

~ * ~

That Thursday before the party, Scott was again invited to dinner at Clay and Julie's place. He walked out of his apartment to look toward the far end of the development. While he was there, Arthur came out of his apartment.

"Hi, Scott. Going on a date?"

"No, I've been invited to my friends' place."

"Good; you should socialize outside of these apartments."

Even though he looked at Arthur as he spoke, Scott glanced at times across the building, but Arthur noticed his changing gaze.

"Are you looking for something or maybe someone?"

"I see why they call you the local gossip. I guess your occupation makes you inquisitive."

"Observant is a better word, plus I have little to do outside of work."

"There's no scoop about me, so I'm going." He tapped Arthur's arm as he left.

Pulling up to the small, single-level house, Scott stayed in his car for a few minutes, reflecting on Arthur's teasing question: What was he looking for? Was it Melinda? He got out, walked to the front door after passing a lawn divided by a concrete walkway, and rang the front door. Julie opened the door, throwing her arms around him.

"It's good to see you," she said. Stepping back, she looked at him. "I have to feed you. You're not very capable in the kitchen; I assumed you've been eating out or ordering takeout. That food is hardly nutritious or calorie-free. Have you lost weight?"

"I haven't been at the apartment that long, nor has it been long since I last saw you. I am tired of fried eggs and grilled cheese sandwiches, the extent of my cooking skills, so I do eat out. But you don't have to feel obligated to feed me. Also, the apartment complex has its version of a Welcome Wagon, and they bring meals, just one so far."

"I bet they're all young women drawn to an attractive young officer."

"Especially one," Clay said as he exited the bedroom.

She looked toward both men, the confusion clear on her face. "What are you talking about, Clay?"

"A very pretty young woman who caught Scott's eye lives in a nearby apartment."

"Is that true, Scottie? Actually, don't tell me. I have to get dinner ready and want to hear about this attractive woman who I assume is unmarried."

"She's single, the only one in the development. There's nothing between us. She's not attracted to me because I'm an officer; no one knows, remember."

"There is more to this whole story, but we can discuss it at the table."

She took the bottle of wine from his hand, gave it to Clay, and said, "Why don't you pour a glass for all three of us. I'm making your favorite, Scottie, Chicken Francese. Hopefully, the meal is as good as the Welcome Wagon's cooking."

Scott and Clay went into the living room. They sat on the patterned chairs, holding their wine glasses. Looking around, Scott said, "This is really nice, not cookie-cutter like my apartment. Looks like Julie has made some changes since last time. I would describe this house as cozy. You know, you saw the apartment in comparison."

"We're happy. It's not too expensive; we can afford the place between the money we got at the wedding, my pay, the Navy's housing allowance, adding in Julie's salary."

Julie called them to gather at the table. A bowl of string beans was at the center next to a small tray of sliced carrots. Julie brought in the meat, positioning it between the vegetables.

"Help yourself, boys; I cook but don't serve. Scottie, you get the first selection of chicken."

Clay murmured, "Guess the honeymoon is over."

They ate saying little, but at the end of the meal, Scott said, "Julie, this is great. I can't wait to see what dessert is."

"Hold on, neither of you is getting a piece of my pie until someone tells me about this beautiful, single young woman."

Clay pointed to Scott to answer.

"There is nothing to tell. Melinda is a bright, outgoing, attractive woman, but we're just friends."

"You've discussed the nature of your relationship with her?"

"Yes. We were sitting by the pool, and she said people in the complex were assuming we would start dating, but we agreed that we were both only there for a short time, so we shouldn't get involved. In addition, she had ended a relationship with a long-term boyfriend and wasn't ready to be in a romantic involvement. We're friends, that's all, end of story."

"Hmm, who first brought up the issue of defining your relationship?" Julie asked.

"She did; why does that matter?" Scott asked.

"Because that means she was thinking about it before you two defined how things were to be between you. Men are so dense."

"You saw her in a bathing suit?" Clay asked.

Scott heard the sound of leather against bone. "Ow," Clay said.

"Did you tell her about my maid of honor?"

Scott frowned in response.

"Sorry, sorry, but seems like a lot has happened since the last time you were here," Julie said. "The interrogation is over, but if you like her..."

"I think I've earned dessert now," Scott said.

Both men helped bring the plates and dishes into the kitchen. Julie shooed them into the living room to wait. Ten minutes later, they reassembled at the table, and Julie handled out plates with a cake slice to each.

While they ate, Clay asked Scott, "Can you keep your rank secret much longer?"

Julie interjected, "I still don't understand this line between officers and enlisted. I talked to their wives when I dropped Clay off at the school when his car was being repaired. They were delightful women. I don't mean to focus on the issue, sorry."

"It's been challenging. I've met a few residents, and one guy said he wondered why he'd never seen me at the school. When I mentioned my class building, which is separate from the main campus, he said he understood why we've never run into each other, considering the short lunch break we get. Another guy jokingly said that he's never seen me in uniform. Therefore, I must be a spy. My biggest challenge will be at the party this weekend that Melinda mentioned."

Julie said, "Melinda mentioned?"

"I walked right into that, didn't I?"

"I think you both are fooling yourselves. There is potential beyond friendship."

Looking at Clay," Scott asked, "Did you know she was clairvoyant when you married her?"

"Don't ask for another piece of cake, wise guy," Julie said.

~ * ~

On Saturday, Scott knew the party was starting by the noise coming from the center of the apartment complex. Dressed in shorts and a T-shirt, he came out of his apartment carrying a case of beer. When he approached the party's center, some of the men cheered. Doors were opening, and couples exited with plastic trays of food. Soon, the tables set up earlier were filled with hot dogs, chips, nuts, and home-baked goods. Scott left the beer to head back to his apartment, reemerging with three six-packs of soda.

"I heard that not all women like beer." A very pregnant woman walked over and hugged Scott, who had to lean forward for the embrace. Scott saw Melinda standing near her doorway, smiling. Over the next few hours, Scott met with a number of residents; most of the men asked the same question: what language was he taking, and what might be his duty station after completing the course? He was pleased that the development's rule for avoiding mention of ratings was followed.

A couple approached him, both with an appearance different from all the others. They had long hair parted in the center, touching their shoulders; she wore a shirt that stopped just below her breasts, leaving her midriff bare, a beaded belt, and faded denim jeans. Her features were small: tiny ears, a delicate nose, and a round mouth. He was tall and gangly; unlike her, his ears protruded from under his hair, and his grin revealed a crooked front tooth. His clothing consisted of jeans, a dark shirt, and a leather vest.

"You must be Jeff and Debbie," Scott said.

"How did you guess? Was my haircut a giveaway?" Jeff said, chortling.

"He lives next to Arthur." Melinda, who approached and touched Scott's arm, said.

Jeff said. "Arthur calls us the hippie couple. That term would best suit our parents. In fact, this vest was my father's. They're living on a farm, growing vegetables, raising animals, a real throw-back lifestyle."

Debbie added, "We would like to live the same lifestyle someday."

Scott watched Melinda walk back toward her sister. She took a tray from Diane's arms, placing it on one of the tables.

Debbie, noticing the movement of Scott's eyes, said, "She a pretty woman."

Music blared from a radio in front of an apartment, but the chatter covered the sound. When Scott saw Melinda again, he walked toward her, but before he could reach her, three men approached him; he recognized Luke, the sailor who lived in the apartment shared with Melinda and her sister.

"Scott, there is a tradition at our parties that the newest community member gets thrown in the pool," Luke said.

The two other men with him grabbed Scott's arm and pulled him toward the pool's edge. Scott didn't resist. When they reached the concrete end, he was given a moment to remove his shoes. They pushed him into the pool and the crowd cheered him on as he trod water. Out of the corner of his eyes, he saw the scene repeated, but this time, three women, one being Diane, walked toward the next victim. At the same time, Luke announced, "We also initiate the most recent female arrival, and that's my sister-in-law, Melinda."

She protested half-heartedly. Melinda flew into the pool wearing white shorts and a light-yellow top. Scott swam toward her. She saw him as she cleared the water from her eyes.

"Did you know this would happen?" Scott asked.

Melinda shook her head. "No, I'm going to kill my sister."

Scott got out of the pool first, extending his hand to Melinda. Once outside the pool, they looked at each other but were interrupted by Diane charging toward her sibling. She wrapped the towel around her sister's waist, whispering, "Those pants are nearly transparent when wet." Melinda blushed as they headed toward their apartment. "We'll be back," Diane called out.

"I'm going to change," Scott said to no one.

Within a few minutes, they were all back at the party. Scott's hair was slicked back, still wet. Melinda came out to find him.

"I guess we're officially members of the complex." Lifting her arm to her face, she added, "I smell of chlorine."

"We seem to have been thrown together, literally this time. You still look great, even if slightly waterlogged."

The radio volume had been raised, and some couples were dancing in the concrete space around the pool. Jeff and Denise shuffled toward them.

"Come on, kids, join in; you deserve it after being inducted."

Scott took Melinda's hand, and they danced, swaying to the lively music. When the song ended, the following was a ballad. Couples around them moved together. Melinda put her hand on the back of his neck while he took her other hand; they pressed close to each other. She giggled in his ear. "The local rumor mill will be very active tomorrow. It's a good thing Arthur isn't here. Otherwise, we could be a featured story in his newspaper."

When the music stopped, Luke came over to them. "Thanks for being a good sport, both of you. Scott, the case you brought was chilled. How did you do that?"

"There's a liquor store about a mile away, and I called them earlier saying I needed a cold case of beer, which they chilled for me. We had parties in the house where I lived previously; I was often the guy to find the best liquor stores. Any reason for your question?"

"Besides your gift, a few others bought beer, usually only a six-pack. We're running out."

"I can drive to the same place, but I had to preorder the chilled case; they have only six packs in their large refrigerator."

"You shouldn't have to pay for more," Luke said. "I'll get other guys to chip in."

"I don't mind. It's the least I can do since I was honored today," he said, smiling.

"Thanks, pal," Luke said, slapping Scott's back.

"Would you go with me?" Scott asked Melinda.

They left together, taking the rear exit. When they neared his car, Melinda stopped. "That's a nice car, a Camaro. I bet it's fast. You park it in the back, so I've never seen it. How can you afford a car like this? What are you, a petty officer third class, second class?"

"My parents paid for college I and worked summers to save. You wouldn't be so impressed if you saw my monthly loan charges. We are still on building grounds; remember the rules: no mentioning military rank." Scott said, "Do you want to drive?"

Her face lit up as he handed the keys to her. Once in the driver's seat, she took hold of the steering wheel. Pulling out of the parking lot, she gunned the engine, and the screech sliced through the quiet.

"I bet they heard that at the party, even with the music and conversations."

"That's okay because they'll think *you're* the reckless one."

On the way back to the apartment complex, Scott said. "Have you had much chance to see all the sights around here? I've been in the area for a while, living in a house before coming here, so I've had the opportunity to explore."

"Why did you leave the house?"

"I had two roommates... one shipped out, and the other got married."

"Okay, second question: why did you ask about the local sights?"

"I heard the weather is nice tomorrow, and I wanted to drive to Carmel. The town is beautiful, and the small beach is not crowded. Why don't you join me?"

"Sure, but as friends, right?"

When they got back to the development, Scott put the beer on the table and took Melinda's hand. The music playing was soft, and they danced slowly. After the music stopped, they stayed close together for a moment.

"I'd better get my rest because I have a non-date tomorrow," Melinda said.

At midday, Scott met Melinda by the pool, and they walked to his car. The drive to Carmel by the Sea was short. Entering shops along the main and side streets, Melinda bought items mostly for her sister. Scott offered to pay, but she refused. They had a late lunch before heading to Ocean Avenue, the road to the beach. Scott took a blanket from the trunk of his car so they could sit on the sand. They reached the ocean's edge by a ramp over a mound of sand. Families with children were scattered about, a few daring to enter the churning water. Scott put the blanket in an area away from most.

"This is so beautiful, Scott; I've had a wonderful time today. Thank you." She squeezed his arm.

For a while, they looked at the roaring ocean, saying nothing.

"Melinda, I don't want to reopen a wound, but what was your ex-boyfriend like; why did you break off with him?"

"I mentioned once before that we practically grew up together, but the connection wasn't romantic until our mid-teens. Unlike many couples, the separation caused by going to different colleges seemed to strengthen the relationship, even though we'd agreed to see others. When we were together later, I knew I could trust him. My father lied to my mother; he cheated on her. Trust, which naturally includes honesty, is essential in any relationship I would have. I've had a few other boyfriends in college, but they either cheated on me or lied."

"Like your father."

"Yes. I guess my relationships, including with my dad, influenced what I value, but I think women want both, as men probably want the same things. My folks divorced; later, my father regretted his actions, but it was too late to heal the marriage. He's good to me and Diane. His interactions with my mother are cordial. Neither remarried, which shows that the damage from dishonesty may never heal. I think she might have eventually forgiven him about the affair if he'd told her. Instead, she heard it from someone else."

"Would it be hard to forgive someone who lied to you even if the deceit was for a reason?"

"I never held it against my parents for telling me Santa Claus was real, but," her expression changed, "adults shouldn't lie to each other no matter how hard it is. Sometimes, people get caught up in a lie and don't know how to escape it. I saw that with a college roommate. I won't ask if you ever lied to someone you were involved with. I don't want my regard for you to change."

"You never answered the second question: why did you break up with the guy? Was the breakup so hurtful that you had to leave your job to come here to live with your sister?"

Melinda said nothing; tears formed on the edge of her eyes.

"I'm so sorry, Melinda. I've asked too many sensitive questions. I have no right to probe your personal life that way. Please forgive me." He reached into his pocket for his handkerchief.

"It's okay. I said that I valued honesty, but I wasn't being honest with you, at least by omission. Teddy, my former boyfriend, actually my fiancé, died. He was driving when a drunk driver hit him. He passed away from his injuries. I needed to get away."

"Oh, god, I'm very sorry." He put his arm around her shoulders.

"Last night, I thought about being with you today, mulling over what I would tell you, not wanting to have a heavy discussion with someone I barely knew."

"I'm glad you told me."

"Me, too."

Scott jumped up and took off his shoes. "Let's stick our feet in the water."

Melinda slipped out of her shoes; Scott grabbed her hand to pull her up, keeping his grip as they stopped at the beach's edge after the overturned waves had lost their strength. The sun was at eye level as they stared out, except when they looked at each other.

"I was at this beach not long ago with a bridesmaid at my friends' wedding."

"Scott, since we're talking about honesty, I admit that despite our agreement not to get involved, I struggle against that commitment, especially now when..."

"We have to stick with it for the reasons we discussed," he said, finishing her sentence, "but as long as we're honest, I'm fighting against wanting more with you. I hope I never do anything that would jeopardize what we have now."

On the way back, Scott took a roundabout trip, passing a group of buildings nearly surrounded by trees.

"I've been by these buildings to the right and wondered what they are. Do you know?" Melinda asked.

"That's the grounds of the Naval Postgraduate School. Officers go there for their masters, mostly in engineering and related disciplines."

"Can we go in there?"

"Sure, it's not a military base."

They drove toward the central building, which was fronted by a large pool. At another section, Melinda pointed toward a sand-colored structure.

"That looks more like a hotel than a classroom," Melinda said.

"That's the Hotel Del Monte," Scott explained.

"How do you know so much about this place?"

Scott paused. "I researched the area when I got my orders to come here."

"Last night, I told my brother-in-law you have a degree and asked if you can get an officer's commission. He said the Navy had several ways for you to look into it, although the way Luke talks, officers are all idiots."

"I know we had lunch late, but are you hungry?"

"No, I'm fine. I should help Diane with dinner. Next time."

An hour later, he'd settled into his apartment, having changed into shorts and a t-shirt. There was a knock at the door. He was surprised to see Melinda.

"Diane wants to invite you for dinner unless you have already eaten; she said there is more than enough. You need to give me your phone number so I can call you rather than knocking on your door. Here's mine, or actually Diane's."

"Okay, but should I bring anything, maybe run to the liquor store to get a bottle of wine after I change?"

"No need, we have wine. Are you coming? I'll wait until you change."

Walking to her place, Scott said, "I had a good time today."

"I did, too. That was one of the best non-dates I've had."

Diane greeted Scott with a hug, and Luke shook his hand.

Luke said, "You were a good sport with the dunking. We expected you would take it well. My sister-in-law didn't respond the same. I heard about it."

"You did not!" Melinda protested.

"No fighting, you two; why don't you help me set the table, sis," Diane said.

Luke said, "I tease Melinda all the time, but I'm fond of her. She can dish it out as well. I'll miss her when she goes home."

"Has Melinda given you guys a date when she's going home?"

Luke shook his head. He yelled into the kitchen, "Diane, can you get us beers?"

"No," Diane called from the kitchen, "we're having wine with a roast; beer goes with hamburgers and hot dogs."

At dinner, Scott sat next to Melinda at the small table, their legs occasionally pressing.

"Melinda mentioned you took her to Carmel and the post-graduate school. I've never been to Carmel or the college," Diane said.

Scott said, "We just drove through the school but didn't go inside any of the buildings."

"That's a school for officers, and I hear the dining room there is great. Officers have all the best, unlike us enlisted," Luke said.

Scott was tempted to defend his rank but held back.

"Are you going to re-enlist when the time comes?" Luke asked.

"I haven't decided; I have plenty of time to make up my mind."

"Aren't you violating the code of not talking about the Navy while we are at the apartments?" Melinda asked haughtily.

"Ha," Luke said, "you forget one of the exceptions is our next duty station, which can mean future enlistment."

"Scott, I'm glad you're a witness to what I have to put up with. These two banter all the time. If I didn't know better, I would think they didn't like each other," Diane said.

"He's all right," Melinda said, putting down her fork.

"She's tolerable," Luke countered. They were smiling at each other.

"Do you have siblings?" Diane asked.

"Yes, a sister. She was adopted; Lilly's in college and graduating soon."

"You never told me you had a sister," Melinda said.

"You'd like her; in some ways, you remind me of Lilly."

"Feisty, I bet," Diane interjected. The dinner was over when she said, "Luke, can help me clear the table. You two can sit by the pool until dessert is ready."

Scott and Melinda sat on chairs near the pool's edge. The moon was above the building; stars gathered across the early night sky. Lights from the apartments were the source of ground-level illumination.

"You're a good listener, and you know much about me, but I realize I know little about you, for example, that you have a sister. What other secrets are you keeping?"

"I'm an open book, ask away."

"Okay, let's start with a simple question: what was your major in college?"

"I studied Asian history and economics."

"Interesting; next question: what is your family like?"

"My parents are still married; my father is an engineer, and my mother teaches art at a local primary school. I've told you about my sister. I had a normal childhood, attentive parents, loads of aunts, uncles, and cousins."

"Now for the tough one: Were you ever in a significant relationship? I told you about mine."

"No, not what I would call significant, certainly not as you experienced. I had girlfriends, some lasting for a while, but they ended without much hurt or regret."

"There has to have been something in your life that significantly impacted you, some major event that influenced you."

"Melinda, I'm an ordinary guy with a boring life. I hope that doesn't chase you away."

"No, I like you for what you are now; I wouldn't call you ordinary, but there is something there that you're not admitting, and I'm going find out. You can't be a criminal, or you wouldn't have gotten in the Navy," she chuckled.

"I guess that means we'll have to spend more time together so you can question me further."

Before Melinda could say anything, Diane was at the door calling them in for dessert.

Two

During the week, Scott replayed Melinda's words in his mind, suggesting that he was withholding something secret. He was bothered about the lie as well as the constant threat that he would be discovered. At times, in language school, he saw other men who lived in the apartments from a distance, and he hurried to avoid them. So far, his walk from the apartment to his car while in uniform was safe, but for how long? What would happen if he revealed his rank? Would that upset the residents at the complex, especially Melinda? Scott knew he could deal with losing local friendships, but losing Melinda was difficult to accept. But what did that mean about his feelings toward her?

A few days later, Scott called, and Diane answered the phone.

"Hi, Diane; is Melinda there?"

Melinda got on the phone. "Hi, Scott, I'm glad you called. What's up?"

"I wanted to ask if you'd join me on a visit to a few wineries along Route 101, assuming you are old enough to be served," he joked.

"Very funny. I'm probably your age or a bit younger, which is something else I don't know about you. We can discuss that at another time. I want to go with you, although it sounds like a date?"

"No, we are just going to sample a few wines together, that's all. If you agree, we can leave on Saturday. I'm in a rut between attending class and studying at the apartment; I need to get out. I suspect you must get bored at times."

"Then it's not a date, since we are going due to boredom. What time?"

As promised, he got to their apartment at one, and before he could greet Diane and Luke, Melinda grabbed his arm and pulled him away from the door. They went to the rear parking area, stopping in front of his car.

"No, you are not driving. There are still tire marks on the road just outside the apartments. I got blamed for the black streaks."

Before they pulled out, Scott stopped. "Are you okay? You didn't say anything to my remark about your driving. I don't know you well, I admit, but I sense you always have a retort unless you are thinking about something else."

"After our phone call, Diane said, 'Are you sure that's a good idea? You two are getting too attached. Several people in the development have been asking if you and Scott were together.'"

"She didn't seem to mind my having dinner with all of you. She encouraged us to go outside after the meal in view of anyone around."

"She likes you but perhaps senses an attraction."

"What did you say?"

"I said she needn't worry. I was tempted to tell her to mind her own business. Besides, who else can I play with? Then she asked if I thought about returning home; if not, what were my reasons?"

Scott put the car in reverse and pulled into the parking lot.

"What are you doing?" Melinda asked.

"You've been through a lot, experiencing emotions I don't know fully but hope to. I don't want to be the reason for any more stress in your life, nor do I want to cause a rift between you and your sister. While you were preparing the food, Luke said he would miss you when you left. I'm sure Diane will miss you even more so. She's just concerned for you."

"I appreciate your words, but you are doing what she does. I can make decisions; I can choose who I want to be with or when I want to leave. Is there more going on here than I know or admit? I can't be certain, but let's not pretend a simple wine tour is the start of a romance. I like you, Scott, I told you that, plus I enjoy your company. We can't let the few words my sister says deter us. More importantly, I want to always be upfront about what people say about us, especially my family, not holding back to avoid upsetting you. So, drive on, buster. Unless you would rather I drive," she added, grinning.

As he pulled out quickly, Scott said, "I like you, too."

"I'm sorry, I didn't hear what you said."

The drive to the wineries took them to the major coast road, Highway 101, which stretched from Oregon to Los Angeles and was the more common route than the precipitous and beautiful Highway One, which overlooked the ocean and climbed the mountainous edge. Pulling up to the first winery, Scott parked on the graveled lot. Before entering the wood-walled testing room, they looked at the rows of grapes, the thick, stretching vines holding the ripening fruit covered by protective leaves. Still moist from the burned-off fog, the grapes glistened in the afternoon sun.

Once inside, they saw rows of bottles lined up on a long counter divided into red and white wine sections. The bar was at the center of the room; couples were leaning over the wooden counter, sipping the small amount in their glasses, tasting samplings. Scott and Melinda approached the bar; a woman wearing a t-shirt with the winery logo placed glasses in front of them. They started with the whites, jotting down their assessment on a provided notepad.

"What do you think, Scott?"

"I prefer the Chardonnay, how about you?"

"I like the Riesling."

They switched to the reds, trying four variations before they finished. Scott bought three bottles, including a Riesling. After leaving the tasting room, they leaned against his car.

"Do our wine preferences say something about us?" Melinda asked. "The fact that you like the full-bodied white and I like the sweeter wines."

"I don't think about our differences, only how we are alike."

"Oh really, tell me how we are similar?"

"We're both college graduates, which allows us to say we are smart, plus..."

"You're half right," Melinda said. "But we are so different. Our family lives are not similar."

"We both have a sister we are close to."

They visited another nearby winery, going through a similar tasting process before leaving, except that Melinda only tasted two whites.

"There's another winery down the road. I'm not sure we should go any further than that. I'll be too drunk to take us home. You're not listening—are you still thinking about what Diane said? I got the message that you can make up your own mind, but does what others think, including your sister, bother you?"

"Maybe, but I'm not going to be in California much longer; as a result, I can't be concerned with rumors or my sister's opinion. I enjoy your company; you know the area better than I do. Is the concept of a friendship between a man and woman so foreign to others?"

"What was your job like back home?"

She stared at him. "You're changing the subject. As I told you, after college, I got an entry-level job in human resources at a nearby distribution center. I hire workers, deal with employees' issues, and handle new staff orientation. I love what I do and hopefully will go back to it in the near future. I won't ask you what your job will be after you finish the course since it is all so secret, Luke says."

"Are you ready to go to the next winery?"

Melinda said, "Sure, but I hope they have something to eat there, even pretzels. I didn't have much for lunch."

"We passed a restaurant a few miles back; we can have an early dinner there."

The restaurant was a simple structure with a posting of the offerings on a painted sign in front. A busy waitress pointed toward a table. The woman who had directed them came to their table carrying menus. Mumbling through the specials, she hurriedly left for a table where a couple was waving to get her attention.

Melinda said, "One year during the summer recess, I worked at a restaurant similar to this but was a terrible waitress. Twice, I dropped plates, took down the wrong order a few times, brought the wrong meal to a table. I would have been fired if the owner wasn't a relative."

"I can't picture you with a pencil behind your ear, smiling obsequiously at an indecisive couple staring at the menu."

"Obsequiously! You are a college graduate."

"Didn't they teach you big words at your college?"

"Sure, I guess I'm not as erudite as you. What kind of jobs did you have?"

"I did okay in my summer jobs, but when I was a kid, I had a paper route. One time, I hit a homeowner in the head with rolled-up paper, threw the thick Sunday edition so hard I broke a window and dented a parked car with my bike. I didn't earn much since my parents said I had to pay for repairs from my tips."

"Good thing we chose different careers now," she said, leaning forward. "I'm glad we did this today. I don't know if it's the wine talking—*in vino veritas*—but this is fun."

They ordered dinner, and Scott asked for a glass of wine while Melinda ordered carbonated water with her meal. It was getting dark by the time they left the restaurant. Outside, they walked to his car, and when they neared, Scott said, "It's too late to go to a third winery."

Melinda touched Scott's arm. "I'm not trying to trick you into letting me drive, but you had wine at the wineries and with dinner. I'm concerned your alcohol level might be too high if we get stopped. You could lose your secret clearance if you get arrested for DUI, right? I drank water with the meal. Would it be best if I drive?"

Scott looked at her for a moment before handing her the keys. Melinda pulled out of the parking lot slowly onto the road. She followed the signs to Highway 101 and entered the freeway. Staying parallel with the speed of the other cars on the road, she soon noticed a stretch of highway where the traffic had thinned. Scott saw a smile forming on her face; before he could say anything, she pressed the accelerator, and the car leaped forward.

"Slow down," Scott yelled, his voice drowned out by the engine's roar.

They'd traveled a few miles before they heard a siren coming from behind them.

"Oh, shit," Melinda said as she slowed. Within a few minutes, a police car pulled behind them, the revolving light reflecting off the rearview mirror and lighting up the interior. A police officer got out to approach Scott's vehicle.

"You were ten miles over the speed limit, young lady. I need to see your license and registration."

While Melinda yanked her license from her wallet, Scott removed the registration from the glove compartment. The officer looked at both documents and then at the two occupants. Leaning across the open window, he spoke to Scott.

"Obviously, this is your car. Letting her drive may not have been the best decision." He paused. "You have a base sticker on the windshield, so you must be active-duty military. For your benefit, I'm not going to ticket this young woman, who is not from this area, based on her license. Ms. Jenkins, consider this a warning."

He headed back to his patrol car.

Melinda waited for a few minutes. "That would have been a memorable way to end the evening."

"Would have been even more memorable if you were jailed."

Melinda drove more slowly to the apartments. Parking in the rear lot, she was still exhilarated when they got out of the car. "Getting pulled over was the highlight of the evening. I was tempted to speed up instead of stopping."

Standing in front of Scott, she reached up and kissed him. He touched her arms.

"I'm sorry, I'm sorry," she repeated. "I shouldn't have done that. I'm sorry."

Melinda, don't..."

She interrupted. "I'm going ahead." She opened her mouth to say something more but decided against it. She walked hurriedly toward her apartment.

~ * ~

The following Wednesday, Scott's class ended at midday, and he decided to go shopping at the Army commissary at Fort Ord in Monterey. Skipping the gym and the opportunity to change out of uniform, he took off his shirt in the car, tucking his foldable garrison cap into his pants pocket. Moving quickly, he turned the corner of the apartment complex, opened his door, jumping inside. Changing into jeans and a long-sleeved shirt, he left, but as he was locking his apartment, he saw Diane and Melinda approach.

"Hi, Scott," Diane said. "You seem to be in a hurry."

"I'm going to the commissary to get some food; my cabinets and refrigerator are bare."

"That's where we're going after we pick up some stuff at the exchange. Why don't you go with us if you don't mind going to the exchange first? There's plenty of room in my car, and since I have a station wagon, we have plenty of space for all our packages. Maybe we can help you pick out more nutritious stuff than you probably do."

"No, thanks for the offer. I want to get back quickly to study for an exam tomorrow."

"One car will save on gas," Melinda said.

"Perhaps some other time, and if you'll excuse me, ladies, I'll be going."

"Maybe we'll see you at the commissary," Melinda called after him.

Scott asked, "How will you get on the base, Melinda? You're not in the Navy."

Diane answered, "Luke got her a temporary pass."

"Okay, maybe I will see you at the commissary." He walked in wide steps to the exit near his apartment.

A few hours later, he looked out the window and saw Melinda walking toward his apartment. He stepped outside to greet her but sensed she was angry.

"What was that all about?" she asked huffily.

"Because I didn't want to go on base with you?"

"We talked about the speculation about us; don't you think your odd behavior adds to it? On the way to the commissary, Diane asked why you were acting so strangely. It seemed logical that you would go with us since we were all going to the same place."

"What did you say to that? Wait! Before you answer, let's go into my apartment so we're not being overheard."

Once inside, she stood while answering. "I told her I was the reason for the snub because you were probably upset with me, sharing that after we went to the wineries, had dinner, and got pulled over by the police, I kissed you in our parking lot."

"I think we'd better sit down; this is getting interesting. What did she say?"

"She said, quote: 'Whoa! That's a loaded statement; start with getting pulled over.' I explained that, with our meal, I drank club soda while you had wine, plus at the tastings in two wineries. I told her I convinced you I'd better drive home. I said I got carried away, speeding on a straight stretch of highway. The police officer just gave me a warning."

"She was content with the explanation?"

"No, she said my story may have explained one part but not the kiss."

Scott said, "This is intriguing. Let me get you a glass of wine."

He left the living room, coming back with two glasses of red wine. Handing one to her, he said, "This came from the winery we visited. Now, go on."

"You're really enjoying my discomfort, aren't you?"

Scott nodded. "Please continue."

"I told her I had an enjoyable time and was perhaps still a bit pumped up about being stopped by the police. In my exuberance, I kissed you, catching you off guard. I emphasized that we were not on a date, The kiss was mild. I said you were probably avoiding me because I violated our friendship agreement. Maybe you felt the ride to the commissary would have been awkward."

"So that was the end of the discussion?" Scott asked.

Melinda sipped from the glass. "I don't think she bought that answer. It was truthful but reflected my confusion. We did look for you at the commissary, but you weren't there."

"Okay, first, I wasn't avoiding you. Second, you surprised me with the kiss, but I was pleased by the affection. I wanted to talk to you alone, without your sister there."

"We're alone now, so say what you want to share."

"We need to stop classifying what we have, friendship or whatever. Let's allow our feelings to develop without worrying about creating impediments or being worried about gossip. I don't know why you kissed me then, but I'm glad you did. If you hadn't, I would have kissed you, if not that night, when we next saw each other."

"Okay, but Diane is going to be watching us, at times, close up."

"What do you mean?"

"You've been invited to dinner tomorrow night again, but there's a purpose this time, so be prepared to be scrutinized if not outright questioned."

"Great, I'll be there."

"If she asks you what kind of relationship we have, what will you say?"

"I'll say what we agreed to, that we have a friendship—right now. I won't add the right now part."

Melinda walked toward the door. "I'd better get back. I'm sure my sister will ask where I was. You said you would kiss me the next time we were together. Does this count?"

Scott kissed her.

~ * ~

Opening his door the next day, he saw Melinda walking out of the apartment complex, twisting car keys around her finger. He marched toward Diane's and Luke's place. Knocking, he was greeted by Diane.

"You're early; come in. Melinda left to pick up some vegetables I forgot to buy at the commissary."

"I thought I would come early so I could talk to you. I know you're concerned about your sister being with me. I assure you I would never do anything to hurt her, especially after she's still recovering from a devastating loss."

"You two would make a great couple, but the timing isn't...."

Luke came out of the bedroom. "Hey, Scott; glad you could make it again."

Diane looked at her husband. "Could you open the wine?" When he walked to the kitchen, she spoke to Scott. "I appreciate you being sensitive to her emotional state, but it's more complex than I can...."

"Hi," Melinda said as she came in the door. "You must be early."

"I told him that. We chatted for a bit before you came," Diane said.

Melinda's eyes moved between the two, squinting until Luke arrived holding two glasses.

"I'll get two more," Luke said, handing one to his wife while Melinda took the other from his hand.

They sat at the dinner table until Diane rose to get the food. "Luke, help me bring in the plates."

Luke said, "Scott, do you know what rank is higher than admiral—a wife, except I don't have to salute her."

Melinda leaned across the table toward Scott. "You had a chat. Was it about me, us?"

"We didn't have much time before Luke walked in, then you arrived."

The dinner consisted of fish and accompanying vegetables. "Melinda cooked the fish and made dessert."

"I need to learn to cook; I hope to have my own place when I return home," Melinda said. She turned her head to return Scott's gaze. "I do have to go home at some time."

"When do you think you'll get your orders, Scott?" Luke asked.

"You know how the Navy operates, hurry up and wait."

"What will you do to fill the time until you have to leave besides study your language?" Melinda asked, biting her lower lip.

"Sis, I think I left the burner on. Could you go with me to get the wine bottle while I check the stove?"

The siblings went into the kitchen—despite attempting to lower her voice, Scott heard Diane's words.

"What are you doing, taunting him?"

"What were you two talking about before I came in? I asked him, but I got a vague answer."

"We both care about you and don't want to see you hurt. I may not have to worry about you two getting close if that's how you treat him; you'll drive him away on your own."

Scott thought he heard a muffled sound when the two women returned, Melinda holding the wine bottle—neither looked at him.

After the meal, Scott thanked his hosts before leaving.

"I'll walk with you," Melinda said, looking at her sister for comment.

"Go ahead. Luke can help me clean up," Diane said.

"I won't be long, promise."

Once outside his apartment, Melinda tugged on Scott's arm. "I'm sorry for my remark. I was annoyed at my sister. She was watching us to measure what we are with each other."

"No need to apologize, but I am curious about the reason. Isn't it obvious I want to go places and do things with you? I thought we wouldn't fight whatever was happening between us. I know you're returning home one day, but I don't understand why you needed to mention it at the table. I realize Diane is not in favor of something developing between us."

"I feel stuck between you and my sister, as well as the current and the future."

"I wish Luke hadn't brought up the issue of my orders— another reminder of limited time, but let's take advantage of those remaining days."

"Do we have plans for the weekend?" she asked sheepishly.

Scott thought for a minute. "Yes, wear jeans. Do you have boots?"

"No, but I'll borrow Diane's. Are we going hiking?"

"Sort of. I'll pick up at eleven."

Three

Scott arrived on time wearing jeans, and low boots. Melinda answered the door wearing similar attire.

"Are you going to tell me where we are going?"

"No, you'll be surprised."

Scott drove past Monterey into Carmel Valley, exiting the main road to a dirt path ending at a large ranch. The house was set back, and the predominant structure was a red-painted barn. A large corral was next to the building; several horses nibbled on the sparse grass.

"Are we riding today?"

A bearded man wearing a cowboy hat approached them. A few yards away, six people had gathered near the corral.

"I'm Scott Oliver. I arranged a ride for two."

While they spoke, a woman came out of the barn holding the reins of two horses. She gave the animals to a couple, after which she repeated her efforts until all those waiting were holding reins.

The man took two horses from the enclosed area, bringing them to Scott and Melinda. Scott's horse was a long-legged gray animal with a white triangle between its eyes and nose. Melinda's ride was a glossy brown with a white mane.

The man commanded, "Everybody mount up." He walked toward Melinda, seeing her puzzled look. "Need help, young lady?"

"I got it," Scott said. He approached Melinda, who was petting the horse's nose. "Get on from the left side by putting your foot into the stirrup while grabbing the horn. Pull on the saddle horn and push up from the stirrup." He put his hands on her waist to hoist her onto the saddle. After she was settled, he mounted his horse.

"My son, Karl, will be leading the group," the owner said, pointing to a young man nodding awkwardly in acknowledgment.

The riders formed a single line and went ahead along a trampled dirt road leading into the woods north of the barn. Melinda held the reins in both hands while gripping the saddle horn.

"I'll stay beside you," Scott said. "The horse will stop if you yank on the reins, or pick up speed if you nudge its sides, but horses are pack animals following the one in front."

After two miles of walking gently, Melinda looked at Scott, "This is nice."

As soon as she finished speaking, the young man in front yelled back, "Now we are going to trot."

The horses picked up pace, the trot's motion jarring the riders. Melinda bounced up on the saddle.

"Ouch," she said. Is this revenge?"

As the hour-long ride was ending, the lead rider slowed along the circular path until the barn was again visible. When the group stopped, Scott dismounted and helped Melinda down.

As they walked to the car, she said, "My butt hurts."

"You're probably bruised; want me to take a look?"

"No," she answered. "Can we walk to the fenced area to look at the horses?"

They leaned over the top of the wood corral and watched the horses move around.

"Oh look," Melinda said, "there's my horse." She pursed her lips to whistle.

The brown animal approached her, settling on the other side of the fencing. Melinda reached over to pet his head.

"I wonder what his name is?"

Scott said, "I heard someone call him Larry."

"That's not a good name. Let's call him Alexander, not Alex, just Alexander."

"Like Alexander the Great."

"Right... like Alexander the Great," she repeated.

"Melinda, are you anxious to leave?"

"No but, I feel confined at the apartments as if I'm in an enclosed area like these horses. I don't have my car to get around; the people at the apartments are wonderful but they're not the friends I've known for a long time, have grown up with. I miss my parents; my job is rewarding. Being with Diane has brought us closer together as sisters. You've been the bright spot. You must feel the same way about being here."

"I've had more time to explore and appreciate the area. You're right—this is not what I signed up for. I'm looking forward to my duty station or ship. I'd be ready to go tomorrow, but for you."

They moved closer together to kiss. Scott felt a shove pushing him away from Melinda as their lips connected.

"Hey, knock it off," he said to the horse.

Melinda roared. "He's jealous."

"Let's move away from the fencing," he said, and they kissed without interruption.

"Buy me a horse, Scott. I can picture my parents' reaction when I drive up with a horse trailer."

"I can envision the response if I ride a horse to my duty station. We may have to hold off."

"I gather you've ridden quite a bit."

"Yes," Scott said. "I grew up in a rural area where horses and paths are plentiful."

"Thank you for today—promise we'll come back."

They held hands as they walked back to his car. Melinda sat gingerly on the passenger side while Scott chuckled softly.

They drove around the area for the rest of the day, eventually stopping in Monterey to dine at a Mexican restaurant. After they left, Scott looked at his watch. "It's early; anything you want to do?"

Melinda pondered while looking around. Her eyes lit up. "There's a nearby place you probably don't know about." Grabbing his hand, "Let's get a beer."

"A beer, we just had—" He didn't complete the sentence, allowing himself to be led.

They stopped in front of a nondescript bar with a flickering light illuminating the pub's name. Once inside, Scott was surprised the bar was crowded. Looking past the people, he saw a raised stage with a microphone set up in the center. The large room smelled of beer and sweat.

"This is a karaoke bar! You're not..."

"It's best to start with alcoholic fortification. I'll buy the beers," Melinda said.

They stood at the bar, Scott slowly drinking while Melinda chugged the beer.

A man stood behind the microphone on the stage, saying, "Anyone else volunteering?"

Melinda pulled Scott's hand so hard he spilled the beer. Before he could say anything, they were on the platform. The man listed the inventory of background music previously taped without vocals.

"Endless Love," Melinda screamed. After a few awkward moments while waiting for the music to start, Scott whispered to Melinda, "I can't sing, plus I don't know the words."

As soon as he said that, the man gave the couple copies of the lyrics.

When the background music began, Melinda started with gusto; Scott hesitated before joining in. Soon, they matched their words, sounding more like a duet. He looked at her and could see she was enjoying the experience. Often during the rendering, she looked at him, smiling. At the end, the crowd clapped politely.

"Wasn't that great? I came here once with Diane and a few of her friends from the apartments on a girls' night out."

On the ride home, Scott said, "You have a nice voice. How did I do?"

Melinda squinted. "The expression, don't give up your day job comes to mind."

At the apartments, Melinda asked, "Will I see you tomorrow?"

"Yes, I have a plan for Sunday."

"You're not going to tell me, are you, even if I bribe you with this?" She put her arms around him, pressing her lips against his.

"I guess we shot the hell out of the friends-only alternative. I also thought I saw several window blinds go up; rumors will heat up," he teased.

~ * ~

Scott picked her up at eleven. He drove to Salinas, passing fields of low vegetables; sprinklers tossed streams of water high to descend as mist.

"I never realized how much there is to see here until you showed me. You're leaving the main road, so we must be near our destination, which you're not explaining."

Scott pulled up into the dirt lot of a long rectangular field of strawberries with a wooden, enclosed stand as the entrance. Green, molded pulp baskets were stacked alongside the temporary structure, and a sign in black letters read three dollars per basket.

"We're going to pick strawberries!"

"Yes, but this is also a contest. Whoever fills the basket last buys dinner."

"You're on."

Scott paid the man inside the stand while Melinda grabbed a basket and began picking from the nearest row.

He yelled, "Hey, you cheated. We should start at the same time."

Ignoring him, Melinda continued pulling the fruit from the plant. Scott raced to gather strawberries, gaining on her as he walked down a parallel row. Looking at her collection, he realized he was slightly ahead, based on the height of the mound in his basket. He felt something strike the side of his head but wasn't stopping to see what hit him until he sensed something dripping down onto his cheek. Swiping at the liquid, he suspected what it was and licked the red drip—strawberry juice. Another bounced off the top of his head—looking at Melinda, he saw her aiming a third at him. With a strawberry already in his hand, he tossed it at her. She fired back; soon, the fruit flew between them until Scott removed a handkerchief from his pocket, waving it in surrender.

They sat in the shade of a section of cut grass under an elm to the left of the patch.

"This is so nice, even though you got stains on my blouse," she said, smiling.

"Melinda, would you mind telling me more about your fiancé, especially how you coped with his death?"

"I've told you what he was like and how our relationship began and grew, leading to marriage plans. I joined my employer while he was starting his career as an architect. One night, he was to pick me up at my parents' house," she took a deep breath.

"You don't have to continue."

"I want to, need to. When he didn't arrive on time, I was worried. I had a feeling something was wrong. The phone rang, and I raced to pick it up. A drunk driver had hit him, and he died at the scene, I was told. Teddy was so careful; he never drank before he got behind the wheel, drove the speed limit, especially when I was in the car." She wiped under her eyes. "I was shattered from that point, couldn't go to work. The funeral was very difficult; the man I loved was in a casket. For a while, I was catatonic. Family and friends helped me get through it, but that wasn't enough, so I came to live with Diane."

Scott touched her arm. "Thank you for sharing that. You needn't go on." She leaned against him when he put his arm around her.

"Who won the strawberry contest?" she asked.

"You were disqualified for cheating, but I'll take you to dinner."

As they stood to leave, Melinda asked, "Why do you need to understand what happened with Teddy?"

"Because it was such a major tragedy in your life, one that likely has changed you. I've never encountered that kind of loss, so I can't draw on my own experience to really understand what you went through. I can only get a glimmer of the pain you felt."

"I thought men didn't want to know or would see me as damaged."

"I have fun with you—you are so full of life, but that's not all of you. I need to understand even the difficulties and heartbreak. But you are *not* damaged."

"Is that all?"

"I need to know if he is the benchmark, the person you will compare me to."

"He was a good man; I won't forget him, but I won't compare you to him."

He hugged her, keeping her in his embrace, ignoring the sounds of children offloading from a bus spewing smoke from its tailpipe.

They ate dinner at a small Chinese restaurant in Monterey. He looked at her between forkfuls with the intensity of sketching.

"Why are you staring at me? Do I still have strawberry stains on my face?"

"No, because you're beautiful." He reached across and took her hand. "I'm not someone who holds much stock in fate, as if what happens in our lives is predestined, not of our own control, but there are so many changes in events that could have kept us from being here now: you could have stayed home despite the loss, never stayed with your sister, I could have found another apartment for the short stay."

"I'm not a believer in fate, either, for obvious reasons," Melinda said. "I don't think I was destined to lose Teddy. But I only know that if I'd not met you, I would have gone home by now."

"That's the elephant in the room, isn't it: when we both leave?"

"Let's leave the pachyderm in the corner for now, okay? I'm weary of what-ifs."

When the waitress came with the dessert list, they stared at each other, having noticed the same thing headlining the list: *strawberry shortcake.*

"You're not going to order that after today, are you? You suddenly have your mischievous look."

"Oh, really; what does that look like?"

Scott screwed up his face but couldn't hold it for long without laughing.

"I am now. We'll have two strawberry shortcakes," she said to the waitress.

Four

Scott accepted Julie's invitation to dinner, showing his appreciation by bringing a bottle of Chianti, having been told they were having an Italian meal, "Not pizza," Julie told him when she offered.

She greeted him at the door with a tight hug. "I'm not just showing affection, I'm seeing if you've lost weight. You pass."

"I'm glad I passed inspection. You, on the other hand—"

Julie released her hold and slapped his arm, "Don't finish that sentence."

Clay walked into the room and said, "I can attest that Julie's the same as when I first met her."

She nodded at her husband and left to go into the kitchen.

Lowering his voice, Clay said, "I'm not an idiot."

"She's still a beauty," Scott said loud enough to be overheard, "and a great cook."

Julie came back into the room and handed Scott the wine opener. "You two don't fool me. Open the bottle and pour into the glasses at the table."

They spoke little while eating the chicken parmigiana, enjoying the meat with spaghetti. When finished, they stayed at the table to talk.

Scott spoke first. "I love coming here, and this is the third time you've invited me, but you don't have to worry about me. You assume I'm not eating well or dining on fast food. I've been eating very well. First, the three women—the Welcome Wagon— bring me dinner periodically, as I mentioned last time. Secondly, I'd been invited to Diane and Luke's for a meal twice. Finally, I've been to a restaurant with Melinda a few times. I feel like all I've been doing lately is being fed."

"Isn't Melinda one of three in the Welcome Wagon and Diane, her sister? Honey, do you sense a common thread in all his meals?" Clay said.

Julie said, "What's the status of your relationship with her?"

Before Scott could answer, Clay added a question: "Have you slept with her yet?"

Julie said, "He slept with my bridesmaid after, what, two days. I'm sure he's bedded Melinda."

"I have not been intimate with her," Scott said.

"I'm sorry, Scottie, we shouldn't tease you about your sex life," Julie said. "Seriously, do you like her?"

"Yes, very much. We're bordering on something very good."

"Are you still getting away with hiding your rank?" Clay asked.

"So far, but it's getting more difficult, and I realize that maintaining a lie requires more lies. For example, Diane and Melinda asked me if I wanted to go with them to the commissary since we were all going there, but I declined, offering some vague reason. I was afraid the guard at the entrance to Fort Ord would ask the occupants to show their ID and would salute when they saw mine, even though I was in civilian clothes."

"See what happens when you lie, Scottie," Julie chimed in. "I don't understand why you maintain the charade."

"Melinda came to my apartment to chew me out for snubbing them. But to suddenly confess, show up in my uniform, or do something else wouldn't go over well. I don't want to mess up things with her while we are getting to know each other. I've met many residents and have a good rapport with them. I don't want to lose that. I get a kick out of their complaints about officers."

"Are you saying, Scottie, that continuing the lie is the real problem, not your rank?"

"That's not quite what I said, but that might be true."

"You men hate to admit you're wrong; even when you do, you soften the admission."

"Okay," Clay said, "Let's get more details on your budding relationship with Melinda."

"Fine, Clay, I wouldn't call it a budding relationship. We started by agreeing to be just friends but have gone past that."

"Have you gone on dates with her?"

Scott paused and looked at the far wall.

"This is going to be interesting," Julie said.

"I took her to the wineries off 101; afterward, we had dinner, and she convinced me that she was the best to drive to the apartments. I'd drunk more wine than she did. On the way back, she got pulled over for speeding; luckily, she didn't get a ticket. When we arrived back, she kissed me."

"And you were appalled by her audacity," Julie said facetiously. "Was that the only time you were with her?"

"I mentioned the invite to her sister's. The next day, we went horseback riding, had dinner at a restaurant, and went to a karaoke bar. The following day, we picked strawberries in Salinas."

"Scottie, I think this is well beyond friendship."

"Julie, there is a bit of incredulity in your tone. I admit we are at another level, but we both recognize obstacles. She is still grieving over her fiancé, who was killed in a car crash. Of course, there is the fact that I'll be leaving in the near future, as all of us have or will. Melinda left her life, including a good job, to be with her sister to heal, but plans to return."

"I don't disbelieve you; I'm annoyed with you because you should be the one who shows restraint by not getting involved with a woman already hurt from a significant loss when you'll be leaving soon and may never see each other again."

"Julie, don't you see the parallel to your relationship with Clay? You had a job you liked, lived with family all around you, and Clay was going into the Navy, which would mean separation. You didn't know about being assigned to language school, which would give you a year together. But when Clay is done at the school, you don't know what lies ahead. Uncertainty is common to most couples when one is in the military."

"Scott, I have to side with my wife. Yes, there was uncertainty for her and me, but you know what will happen soon. Besides, when Julie and I had to make decisions about our lives together, we had developed a deep love. So, going our separate ways wasn't a consideration. You just started your involvement."

"I agree that avoiding getting closer is best, but I also know when my resolve will melt when I see her next. There is another obstacle. Melinda said she and her boyfriend were always candid with each other and that she values honesty. Of course, I've told a big lie, never correcting the deceit when I was with her."

"All women want honesty in their relationship, but the deeper you bury yourself in continuing the act, the more difficult it becomes to salvage what may develop if that's what you want. Just talk to her, Scottie," Julie said.

Looking toward Clay, Scott said, "As you see, your wife has a strong opinion of what I should do—how about you?"

"If you are going to continue, I suggest you wait until there is clearer involvement with Melinda. If you tell her you're an officer, she'll likely share that with others, especially her sister, if keeping the secret still matters at the apartments."

Julie spoke next. "I'll say one more thing before getting dessert. You obviously care for Melinda and are struggling against your feelings for her. I know you've explained why it wouldn't work—you are getting reassigned, and she is going back to her life, but if you both care for each other, the remaining time could be very special, only if you tell her the truth. You could be surprised; she could understand, but not if you continue to keep her in the dark. I understand my dear husband's viewpoint, but if you don't tell her, she'll feel you don't trust her to keep your secret. The longer you keep it from her, the worse the consequences."

During dessert, they didn't talk about Melinda or the deception, but Scott fretted about what to do on the way home.

Five

After class, Scott headed for a swim in the apartment pool. From his front door, he saw a woman taking laps in the water, and as he neared, he realized it was Melinda. Sitting on the concrete edge, he watched her glide back and forth, her arms reaching forward and back and her legs kicking. She saw him and got out of the water. Walking to the side, she said, "You changed into your bathing suit. The pool is wide enough for us both unless you're avoiding me," Melinda said.

"No, I'm not avoiding you. After what we had, how can you say that even as jest."

"I was right; we fed the rumor mill this weekend. Two women in nearby apartments asked if you were my boyfriend."

"We're both single, so what's the big deal? We could really enflame the speculation by making out right now."

"As tempting as that sounds, gossip spreads easily without our encouragement. I prefer not to be the center of discussions at afternoon coffees, but I care for you, and it doesn't matter to me who knows."

"I'm also not bothered by rumors. We are a novelty: two single people in the development of married couples. I would be irked if people think we got together because it was easy, living in nearby apartments."

"We have to be totally honest with each other in deciding what we want to do from now on. I like being with you, enjoyed our touching and kissing, but it can't be in the moment without considering the consequences. What we could mean to each other also scares me. We don't have many weeks to figure it out. Most couples would let a relationship form naturally over time. We don't have that luxury. What should we do?"

Scott looked at the water. "We'll race across the pool, and the loser has to begin the conversation."

"Remember when we started a conversation about our differences and similarities? It's safe to say we are both competitive." Melinda shook his hand in agreement.

In the front of the pool, Melinda said, "Count to three, Scott, and we'll start."

At the end of the count, both leaped into the pool. Midway across the water, he was ahead of her, but Melinda was suddenly in the lead as they turned for the last lap. She swam further away from him, and she touched the other side before he did.

"You beat me," Scott said between taking in air.

"I didn't tell you I swam competitively in college, did I?"

"When do you want to talk?" Scott asked.

"After the party this Sunday, I have to help get ready for Diane's birthday party. It's an open house but will likely spill out to the pool area. You got the invitation: I put them under all the doors. You are going, aren't you? You don't have to bring a present."

"I'll be there."

~ * ~

At school the next day, the instructor, a short, gray-haired man, asked Scott if they could meet in the hallway during the morning break. In their subsequent discussion, the instructor told him Seaman Bristol was struggling with the language.

"As I'm sure you know," the teacher said in an accented but precise speech, "this is the more difficult study section. The seaman memorizes the words but struggles with the intonation. Emphasis on syllables is important in Asian languages, which he doesn't grasp fully. I'm afraid he will fail the next series of exams and the final. His grades so far haven't been good."

"That will change his specialty designator as well as his eventual assignment. I appreciate you telling me."

At the end of the day's class, Scott, the only officer of the fourteen students in the room, said to the instructor that he wanted to meet with the others in the course.

The instructor left the room.

"Seaman Bristol is struggling with the language, as you likely noticed in the class exercises. We need to help him; otherwise, his career with the Navy will change significantly. I'm proposing that we all take a one-hour period with Bristol to focus on pronunciation, Monday through Friday."

Seaman Apprentice Johannson raised his hand. "Sir, is that an order?"

"No, Johannson. How dependable will you be on a ship or duty station if you won't assist a shipmate? If you can't commit time to others, you don't belong in this program or the Navy. Some of you have already been through one tour, and I'm sure you can support what I've said. Petty Officer Reynolds, make a list of volunteers, including the day they are willing to assist. Put me down for tomorrow."

All the students volunteered.

~ * ~

Later that day, Scott called Julie. "I need your help. I was invited to a birthday party for Melinda's sister, and I don't know what to get her for a present. Melinda said a gift wasn't necessary, but...."

Julie interrupted. "You want to impress your girlfriend's sibling."

"She's not my girlfriend, but you are otherwise right. Can you meet me at the mall and help me decide what to buy?"

"Haven't you bought gifts for other young women?"

"Yes, but my sister always helped me. I don't want to take you away from Clay; you married recently and are still in the honeymoon period."

"Scott, we were in the honeymoon period *before* the marriage. I wish I could see you right now... I bet you're blushing. Clay will probably go bowling with friends. Meet me at the mall at one."

The mall outside Monterey was rectangular, with shops lining the interior. Wooden benches were scattered about; kiosks dotted the glossy floor selling t-shirts, perfume, and other products. Scott saw Julie waving from a distance, and they walked toward each other.

"Do you have any thoughts about what you want to get her?" Julie asked.

"No," Scott answered. "I don't want to buy something too expensive, which might seem over the top. I want to get something nice. I don't know her taste and couldn't guess her sizes."

They went into a few stores, including one for women's clothing. Julie headed toward the lingerie section to select a sheer nightgown. "You could buy it for Melinda if not for her sister."

"Very funny—let's get out of here before I'm seen."

After they left the store, Julie pointed to a row of scarves in a window, suggesting he buy one as a gift. At the counter to pay, the saleswoman noticed Julie's wedding band and engagement ring while Scott took out his wallet. "How nice, buying a present for your wife."

Julie took hold of Scott's arm and squeezed. "Thank you, sweetheart."

The woman frowned when he said, "She's not my wife."

Once outside the store, Julie doubled over. "How about I treat you to a cup of coffee and a piece of pie as penance for embarrassing you," she said.

They found a place to order coffee and sat at a Formica table.

"This shop reminds me of something from the fifties," Julie said. "Have you seen Melinda recently and talked more about where things are going?"

"Sort of. We agreed to have an honest discussion soon. I cringe when she uses the word *honest*."

"Scottie, why don't you tell her? I don't know why it's such a big deal. You're an officer—that's something you should be proud of. I've told you my thoughts on this fraternization stuff. This young woman means a great deal to you, and you need someone in your life. Enough said."

"Clay married a wise woman."

"I remind him of that often. I understand the Navy life brings a lot of uncertainty, and separation from friends and people you care about is hard. Clay and I talk about individuals we will miss when we or others leave here with no guarantee we'll ever wind up in the same duty station; that's assuming we make the military our choice in the future. You're on the top of that list for both of us. However, that fact shouldn't keep us from enjoying the company of someone we value now. Sorry. I guess I wasn't done."

He reached across and squeezed her hand. "I should be buying you something."

"You can, another donut."

~ * ~

On the afternoon of the party, Scott left his apartment with the present under his arm. Looking toward Diane and Luke's apartment, he saw people gathering around their front door, which was open with some couples going inside. He followed those entering the apartment, where Diane greeted him, thanking him for coming. He handed her the gift. Scott looked around for Melinda until she came out of the kitchen carrying paper plates, napkins, and plastic forks. He walked toward her; she stopped what she was doing to look at him.

"You didn't have to bring a gift, remember."

"There are many residents here for her birthday. With so many apartments, there must be celebrations all the time."

"No, many couples celebrate birthdays privately or go out to dinner. My sister will be thirty; that's a special one. Also, she knows most couples in the apartments. Luke invited some from his class."

"I'm sure you have a lot to do, so I won't keep you. I'll see you later."

Scott talked to some of those outside, and met couples he hadn't previously, including a young sailor and his wife who had just moved to an apartment on the second level. While he walked around, Debbie showed him a small box holding a beaded necklace she had made for the occasion. Later, Luke brought out a small table, and Melinda followed, carrying a cake with a row of lit candles.

"Everyone," Luke shouted, "Time to sing happy birthday to Diane."

Melinda waved her arms like a band conductor, and the crowd sang in unison, albeit off-key. While her arms were in motion, Melinda's eyes scanned the group until she saw Scott. Over the next few hours, they had brief moments to talk, but when the party ended, Melinda began the cleanup.

<h1 style="text-align:center">Six</h1>

Late Sunday afternoon, Scott considered what he would say to her when they met as planned. Would he tell her how he felt about her, should he reveal his rank? He hoped that if he explained his feelings and wanted the relationship to go further—not sure what that meant—she would respond the same way. But the fact that he is an officer and has been lying since he arrived might defeat any thoughts of a romantic attachment. He knew he was being cowardly, but there was too much to discuss without revealing the lie. The alternative, he thought, was to continue without any declaration of feelings or label on their relationship, but he recognized that he was falling in love with Melinda.

Before going to her apartment, he went outside to put his language books in the car. Looking toward the pool, he saw a woman seated in a webbed chair, leaning over with her head in her hands, her shoulders shaking. Staring at the figure, he suddenly realized it was Melinda. He rushed toward her, but before he could approach her, Diane came out of her apartment, raising the palm of her hand out in his direction. He stopped, waiting for her to draw closer.

"You can't help her right now; you'd only add to her confusion. I'm sure she'll explain everything soon."

Scott returned to his apartment, but he couldn't get the image of her crying out of his mind.

In the evening, he was sitting on the couch when there was a knock on the door. He opened to Melinda on the other side. Her eyes were bloodshot. She sat on the couch and he moved beside her.

She took a deep breath. "This Thursday is the anniversary of Teddy's death." Her voice rose when she started to cry. "What do I call him now: my ex-boyfriend, my former boyfriend, my deceased boyfriend?" She was sobbing.

Scott put his arm around her, and Melinda leaned into him, pressing her face against his shirt, wetting the fabric with her tears.

"His family is having a remembrance beginning with a church service, followed by a ceremony at the grave site. My mother called to remind me of the anniversary, as if I needed a reminder; my parents offered to pay for my trip home. I need to go, Scott."

"When are you leaving? A better question is: Are you coming back?"

"I'm not ready to move home." Looking up at him, she added, "I'm not ready to stay away from you. I'll leave tomorrow. I can't refuse since his parents have asked that I be there."

"Do you want me to drive you to the airport?"

"No, that would make it more difficult. Diane will take me. We never had our talk, did we?"

"That can wait, but I will miss you."

Standing, Scott embraced her again; Melinda's eyes filled.

~ * ~

At eight o'clock, the phone rang. Julie was on the other end.

"How did it go?" she asked. Scott had mentioned the meeting with Melinda.

"Not as I imagined. Before we could talk, she got a call from her parents, offering to pay for her trip home. The anniversary of her former boyfriend's death is later this week, and there is a planned event to mark the date. I can't imagine what's going through her mind."

"I'm sorry, Scottie. I'm sad for her, even though I never met Melinda. I wonder what it will do to any relationship you two might have. She is coming back, isn't she?"

"Melinda said she is, but who really knows? Her family, except her sister, her job, and her life are there. Pacific Grove is temporary. She may decide to stay there."

"I bet she'll come back, but her emotional state will require gentle care if she does."

"Julie, perhaps this brings into focus whether or not we should begin a serious relationship. Melinda has gone through a lot, and if she was getting past the death, the trip back with all its reminders could reignite the sorrows and pain. I was going to tell her how much I cared, that we should take a risk and see where things would go if we got closer. We did discuss it briefly, and she seemed positive. Now I'm not so sure. Time is running out regardless."

"I'm here, Scottie, if you need to talk to me more."

~ * ~

On Wednesday, Scott was completing a run through the local park, having increased his workout routine beginning with the gym. The weather at that time of year was unpredictable: one day of bright, warm days with periodic cooler, overcast days. After changing into shorts and a light sweatshirt, he sat by the pool, staring at the empty water, recalling the times with Melinda. Suddenly, two figures came running out of an apartment, both in bathing suits; Scott recognized Debbie and Jeff as they charged toward the pool, their hands enjoined, yelling as they entered the cold water. Debbie waved to Scott, and he lifted his arm in response. He was about to go into his apartment when he saw Diane carrying a laundry basket. He jogged to her. Upon seeing him approach, Diane put the basket down.

"Have you heard from Melinda?" he asked.

"Yes, I spoke to her and my mother. The service was nice but very difficult for my sister."

"Do you know how long she is staying there?"

"No, but there is a possible chance she won't be coming back. I know my parents are encouraging her to stay. However, I don't know what Melinda is thinking. She's been very evasive; perhaps undecided is a better word when I spoke to her by phone. She asked about you. Scott, it's best that she stays home. I will miss her, but we both need to consider what's best for her. Regardless, I don't believe she'll make up her mind before the end of the week or next."

In the evening, Scott spoke to Julie and relayed his conversation with Diane. On Thursday, Clay called.

"Hey buddy, I wanted to invite you to come over on Saturday to watch the game. I could grill some hot dogs; Julie would make chili. Bring a six-pack of beer. You can stay in the spare bedroom, so you don't have to worry about driving home after drinking."

"Thanks to you both, but I want to get away this weekend. I rented a cabin near the Salinas Valley. From all that I've read, the place is pretty isolated. I can pick up the keys in a grocery store in a neighboring town while buying the few things I'll need."

"I understand. Have you heard anything about your duty station after you finish language classes?"

"No. I contacted the detailer, but nothing yet. I'll give you guys a call when I get back."

Scott left Saturday morning to drive to Salinas, heading west to a hill area beyond the growing fields. As promised, the log cabin was separated from other houses and the paved roads. Tall trees bordered three-quarters of the structure, shading the back, darkening the rear rooms inside. A wide porch, an overhang, a rocking chair, and a wood-burning grill fronted the cabin. Inside, the living room filled much of the interior space with a stone fireplace and rustic furniture that seemed made by a craftsman. The walls were bare; the oak floor was partly covered by scattered thick rugs worn thin by booted feet. The kitchen was basic: a stove, refrigerator, and farmhouse sink. Scott breathed a sigh of relief when he eyed a coffee maker on the chipped marble counter after unloading the packages of food he'd bought. Placing the items in the overhead cabinets above the refrigerator, he went outside to look at the stretch of open land beyond the porch. Most of the ground was bare except for sections of wild grass that grew in formless patterns. In one section, however, there were indications of a long-unattended garden with barely visible burrows in the overturned soil. A deer about five yards away was chomping the grass, leaving stumps of green. Rabbits ran wild, unbothered by his presence; he felt like an intruder to the creatures, unintimidated by his standing there. The sprayed stench from an agitated skunk soiled the air. He could hear the faraway sound of a tractor. The sunlight had snaked around the trees or filtered through the thin leaves.

Sitting on the rocker, he thought about the last few days, Melinda's sudden departure, and Diane's warning that she might not come back to Pacific Grove. Melinda had been on his mind during the drive and at the cabin, despite the fact that the surroundings bore no resemblance to the apartments. He jumped up—his quick motion startled the fleeing deer and chased the rabbits. Wasps circled, causing him to rush into the cabin. As the last stage of settling in, he removed his clothes from his bag and hung them in the bedroom closet. The other room across from the sole bedroom was empty. The floor had a layer of dust and cobwebs built by industrious spiders. Searching the rooms, he noticed no washing appliances: dishwasher, clothes washer/dryer. Attached to the refrigerator was a lined paper that listed a laundromat, nearby restaurants, and local attractions. The house also lacked a television. The single house phone rested on a small table in the living room. Anticipating the lack of TV, Scott had brought two books. Remembering that he'd seen a path curved in the land at the edge of the house, he changed into shorts and began jogging, passing through a dense stretch of woods ending in a nearby stream.

At night, he sat on the couch with one of the novels he had brought but soon became tired of reading and leaned back against the cushion. He pieced together the times with Melinda chronologically, starting with the first time he had seen her sitting by the pool.

The evening sounds consisted of owls, coyotes, other cries, and squawks he couldn't identify. He found the cacophony oddly soothing; his eyes began to close. The bang of the garbage container falling over, and the frustrated grunt of a bear woke him, so he went to bed.

In the morning, he was hungry. Going into the kitchen, he pulled a pan from below the sink, fried two eggs and a slab of bacon. The smell of the sizzling meat increased his hunger, and he ate voraciously.

Seven

After completing a three-hour exam, Scott went home without exercising or changing at the gym. He removed his shirt in the car and rushed into his apartment undetected. He put on shorts and a T-shirt, leaving his uniform in a pile on the bedroom floor. He had fallen asleep on the couch when a knock on the door awakened him... he opened it to Diane and Mariam, both carrying food, Mariam with a pot pie on a tin tray and Diane with a salad in a wooden bowl.

"Come in, ladies, and thank you. I was wondering what I would do for dinner. What, no dessert?" he joked.

Diane looked at Mariam, "Did we forget dessert?"

"I don't think so."

Melinda was standing outside the open front door carrying a tray of cookies.

Scott stood there, his mouth open, staring at Melinda.

"Put everything on the table," Diane said, and the three women placed their meal components on the tabletop. "I assume you have salad dressing, Scott."

He wasn't listening, still stunned by seeing Melinda. "When did you—"

"I'll be back later and will explain," she said softly so the others would not hear.

"Thank you again for the meal and the surprise."

Mariam said, "We need to get back for our own dinner; you're welcome, Scott."

A few hours later, Melinda was at the door. Scott led her to the couch. They faced each other so closely that Scott could feel her breath on his face.

"I need to tell you a great deal, so please don't interrupt, because I'm afraid I'll forget everything I want to say or chicken out," Melinda said.

"I won't say a word."

She inhaled deeply. "As you know, I was invited to commemorate Teddy's death, which consisted of a church service and a visit to the gravesite. After the memorial, we all went to his parents' house. While there, I spoke to his brother Peter—we reminisced about Teddy. He mentioned the accident that killed his brother, reminding me that Teddy was on his way to pick me up when he crashed. I rarely focused on the crash, so traumatized by his death that I blocked out the details." She took a deep breath; tears had formed at the edge of her eyes. "Teddy and I were going to see a play in the city, but I was running late. I called him to let him know. He delayed leaving, but we would likely arrive late at the theater. He must have been speeding to make up the time, as the police report claimed, because of me. I was the cause of his death. I know his brother wasn't blaming me, but I blame myself.

"I was a wreck, but my mom and dad were there to support me. In the midst of all that sorrow and remembrance, I thought of you, which compounded my confusion. How could I start something with someone who could hurt me—not deliberately—by leaving? I wasn't sure I could bear up under that. My parents encouraged me to stay; I was home with everything familiar. I went to my job and enjoyed seeing the people I worked with; my boss pushed me to stay. I called Diane to get my big sister's input and she reminded me that she and Luke would be leaving California in the future, so why come back? Diane is fond of you but doesn't think we are the best for each other right now. Everything and everyone were telling me to stay home, don't go back to Pacific Grove. All that time, I was missing you. Ironically, Teddy's mother was encouraging, even though she didn't know about you, but she warned me not to be stuck in the past and not let Teddy's memory get in the way of a new relationship. I also didn't know your reaction, that is, would I return here and discover you don't want to get involved? I'd understand, but I couldn't have my heart broken again. It was so easy to stay home to avoid the hurt that could come from a relationship that was destined to end and we would be far apart. That was the reasoning part of my brain warning me, but the emotional segment kept telling me to take the risk. I felt like two parts of my head were fighting, and their errant punches were knocking me out. I want to be with you, to know where we will go, but now I need to know how you feel."

Scott explained. "I rented a cabin in the middle of nowhere to get away from the apartment complex where there is so much of you reminding me that I might never see you again. But instead of distracting me, I thought of you in that unfamiliar place with its ants, spiders, and creatures that howl at night. I want to get closer to you, to put my arms around you, kiss you. I need to see you as often as I can. However, I can't deny that we have an uncertain future together or how much we both will be hurt when we are forced to be apart. I suspect if we surveyed the residents, the majority would advise against our relationship forming, but despite all that, I still want to be with you for the time we do have."

"But you really don't know me. You might find I'm not the person you think I am."

"With all the uncertainty of our lives, I'm certain I wouldn't be disappointed by knowing you better, just the opposite."

"We need to go slow right now despite our limited time. I'm still a bit raw, vulnerable from the trip," she said as she slid closer to him.

"You mentioned your parents as if they were together, but I thought you said they divorced."

"They are, however, they got together to comfort me. It was a temporary reunion; they'd been with each other times before, primarily regarding their children. My mother went through a rough period, and I believe she had help in the early years. My father has always been there for Diane and us. I knew my dad had a long-term girlfriend, but I think he still cared for my mother. Both were at the services and beyond, and they jointly purchased my ticket home. They seemed closer than I've seen them in a long time."

"Did you mention us to your folks?"

"To my mother, yes."

"What did she have to say?"

"Both parents want me to be happy, to avoid being hurt, but know me well enough that I need to make my own decisions."

Scott put his arms around her, and they kissed, prolonging the connection. Afterward, Melinda put her head on his shoulder.

"I miss kissing you, even though you initiated our first."

"Better get used to the fact that if you're slow to action, I won't be. I'd better get back to Diane. Will I see you tomorrow?"

"Of course. When I'm done with class. I'll meet you by the pool, and we'll go for a drive."

They kissed quickly before opening the door. Scott stepped out and watched her walk back to the other end of the development.

Eight

The following day, Scott went to the gym solely to change. After dropping his bag inside his apartment, he waited outside until he saw Melinda walk toward the pool chairs. He headed toward her, and they sat near the pool for a while, chatting.

"We spend so much time within this small area; let's get out of here."

They went to the rear parking lot and got into Scott's car, driving a short distance to the rocky edge of the Pacific at Monterey. Scott took a blanket from the trunk, drawing a surprise look from Melinda. Local residents sat on folding chairs, looking at the sea lions resting on the thick rocks.

"These people come out every fair-weather day at this time and stay until it gets dark, sometimes bringing picnic baskets," Scott said as he spread the blanket on the grass. They watched the creatures, who mainly ignored the audience for over an hour.

Some of the watchers folded their chairs after the sea lions slumbered.

"You must be hungry," Scott said.

"I am, but you needn't take me somewhere expensive unless we split the bill. I know what Luke makes, so your pay can't be much more. I still don't know how you can afford your car, apartment rent, food, and other expenses."

"I have a place in mind that is inexpensive."

They traveled to Monterey Wharf, a long pier with a takeout restaurant at the far end. They walked down the weathered wood, hands held until they reached the counter under a canopy. They both ordered fish and chips placed in a conic paper holder, poured salt over the fries, and sat on a nearby bench. Scott went back to get them lemonade.

"You know many places to go to around here; I'm impressed."

"You ain't seen nothin' yet. I have plans. There are places around Monterey as well as north and south of here. I'll take you to all those sites."

"Scott, you don't have to schedule our lives; I want to spend time with you without distractions, without sightseeing. I really don't know much about you. What were you like as a kid? Equally, you don't know much about me."

"Okay, I won't arrange all our time together; I want to know more about you."

"We don't have to see each other every day because I know you must study after class, but the weekend is not always enough."

"Agreed. "We are the source of entertainment in the apartments; I suspect that the more time we spend together, the more rumors will be fed."

"We can be overt with our affection at the apartments; screw the gossip. I want to be able to come to your apartment when you can interrupt your studies, not caring if people who see me enter think we're having sex."

"Speaking of which..."

"Is that your definition of going slow? There will be a time."

After they finished their meal, Scott wiped Melinda's mouth with the end of a napkin. Looking at her, he saw she was staring past him

"Are you okay?"

"The Monteleones, our nearest neighbor, are leaving today. I don't know them well, but their departing reminds me that one day you'll have to go."

"Let's not focus on that except to know that we have to take advantage of whatever time we have together. I still remember that you could have stayed home, and whatever we have, whatever will develop wouldn't have happened."

She kissed his cheek and leaned into him. "I can't believe you went to a remote cabin to get away from me or rather the thoughts of me. A bear could have eaten you," she joked.

"Or I could have been stomped to death by a herd of deer or mauled by a pack of wolves. Maybe I should take you there."

"Let's not get dramatic, and I don't want to go someplace that doesn't have a television."

They arrived at the apartment complex after dark. As they sat in his car, Scott said, "We should say good night here away from prying eyes." They kissed deeply and held each other, reluctant to break away.

Suddenly, Melinda stiffened and ordered, "Get out of the car."

Scott complied, uncertain of her intent. Melinda got out from the other side, walked around the car, and, grabbing his hand, yanked him toward the rear entrance. "We're not hiding that we're together ever again. Everybody knows anyway. Didn't you hear what I told you earlier?" She pulled him to her door. Two couples sat near the pool, the moonlight brightening the green water and lights from the apartments illuminating the area. Melinda threw her arms around him and kissed him, ignoring the stares.

~ * ~

The next day, Scott called her. "I never know who I'm going to get when I call: Diane, Luke, or you."

"You got me; Mom and Dad went out. What's up?"

"I was going to ask you the same question, thinking if you weren't doing anything, we could go for a drive."

"Are you done with homework?"

"Yes, but that's not the reason. I wanted to see you."

"*I'm* doing something," she said, "making cookies. I'm really into baking. You can try one to sample."

"That makes me the guinea pig rather than your sister and her husband."

"If I poison you, only one person dies; if I poison them, two die. It's solely the numbers."

"That's discouraging, but I'll take my chances. I'll need a few minutes before heading there."

Melinda said, "Okay, no need to knock, just come in."

When he entered, Scott saw her sitting on the couch with a book and pen in her hand. He stared at her for a moment. Barefoot, Melinda wore a light gray shirt and a mini-skirt that had risen to midthigh.

"Are you writing a book?" Scott asked.

"Sort of; it's my diary."

"I wouldn't picture you as a diarist."

She squinted. "Oh really; what does one look like?"

Scott blushed. "A ten-year-old jotting in a small pink-covered book with a small lock and key."

"You realize how insulting and sexist that is. I guess males don't keep diaries. Look, no lock."

"Sorry, I was being presumptuous."

"I started writing in this after Teddy died, allowing me to sort my feelings and emotions. You can be dishonest about your mental state, but you can't lie to yourself on paper."

"You mean it's therapeutic—is that what you are writing now, about Teddy?"

"No, writing in this book has also become a habit, a way to record my experiences and responses, so I write down many things."

"Are we, our relationship, now the subject in your diary?"

"It helps me assess my thoughts about us."

"What have you surmised?"

"I haven't yet. The latest section is still a work in progress."

Smiling, he asked, "What do you say about me?"

"It's not only about you, sailor."

"Would you ever let me read what you wrote?"

"No, the book is too personal, plus we're still new. You wouldn't be disappointed by what I've written about you."

"Okay, where are these cookies? Not that I'm anxious to die."

"They're still in the oven for a few more minutes."

"While we're waiting, can I see your room?"

"Why would you want to do that... it's like the spare in your apartment?"

"I don't know, maybe just to envision where you are when you're there."

"If you want but don't get any ideas. I saw you staring at my legs."

They went into her room. Scott scanned the space, his eyes resting on the photograph of Melinda and her family. She jumped on the bed, lying against the pillow covered by the bedspread, looking up at Scott.

He laid down beside her, reaching over to kiss her. She returned the affection.

"I'm trying to get an image of you in pajamas."

"I do wear pj's, not sleep in the nude. There's only one bathroom, remember. It could get embarrassing if I got up in the middle of the night."

"The image of you naked in the hallway is easier to conjure."

"This conversation will lead to trouble; let's get out of here. The cookies should be done."

She leaped from the bedroom, putting her hand out to pull him up.

After she removed the cookies from the oven, Melinda brought a trayful into the living room.

~ * ~

The next afternoon, Scott left Arthur's apartment after dropping off a box wrongly placed in front of his door when he saw Melinda carrying a bag of garbage heading to the parking lot bin. Catching up to her, he offered to take the bag.

"It's not heavy, but you can go with me."

"I'd like to see you tomorrow, and I need to take you somewhere so we can be alone."

"Scott, your place is fine. You still seem to be bothered that everyone knows about us. It won't surprise anyone if I'm seen going in and out of your apartment. We don't need to leave the development or meet by the dumpster. I realize you're trying to protect me—the sister who gets involved with the single sailor before he goes away—it sounds like a sea story. I don't care." She kissed him lightly to reinforce her words. "Besides, we're old news."

"That's fine with me, and I'll skip the gym to get home earlier."

"Oh, no," she said, patting his stomach, "I won't be the cause of you getting flabby. We're eating dinner at five because Diane and Luke have friends coming over to play cards. I'll come down after dinner."

Scott picked up a take-out dinner after the gym, finished the meal, and waited for Melinda. A knock on the door indicated her arrival.

Opening the door, he stood still, staring at Melinda.

"Are you going to let me in?" she asked teasingly.

"Sorry," he explained as she entered, "have I ever told you how beautiful you are?"

"Actually, yes, once, but you can repeat the compliment."

They sat on the couch facing each other; she reached over to kiss him.

"We are no longer the topic for speculation?" Scott asked.

"No. We've been replaced by rumors about the O'Brians, who live two doors from us. They've been arguing a lot and forgot to close their windows. Also, Barbara Sinclair may be pregnant."

He moved closer to Melinda so they could embrace more tightly while her hands went to the back of his head to increase the pressure on their lips. After a while, Scott touched the top button on her blouse and undid it, moving his hand to the next down, and the top of her bra was visible. Once the third button was undone, he reached beneath the cloth to her bound breasts. Melinda stiffened and slid back on the cushions.

"Not yet; I need more time."

Reconnecting the buttons to the holes he said, "I can wait."

Melinda moved back toward him but suddenly stopped.

"Did you hear that?" she said.

Scott listened, detecting the word *Help* repeated. They got up from the couch and opened the front door. The yelling was loud, and apartment doors were opening all across the complex. Soon, residents were surrounding a woman, but at first, Scott couldn't tell who was the cause of the commotion. Debbie stood at the center of the crowd, her braided hair whipping around as she talked to the circle. Getting closer, Scott heard her explain the cause of her anguish. Melinda came up behind him, putting her hands on Scott's back.

"The police arrested Jeff for buying a bag of marijuana, just enough for a few cigarettes. They treated him like he was a drug dealer, placing handcuffs on his wrists, pushing him into the police van, and taking him to the station."

A few people questioned what they could do. Scott looked at the assembled residents.

"Arthur's not here. Could you get him, Melinda?"

She banged on Arthur's door. The older man answered, his hair tousled, his eyes half open.

"I nodded off," he said. Looking past her, he saw the crowd collected near the pool. "What's going on?'

"Jeff's been arrested. Scott asked for you."

Closing the door behind him, Arthur followed her until they reached Scott and Debbie. Scott spoke loud enough for everyone to hear.

"Arthur would be the best person to talk to the police rather than any of us. I suspect you may know many of the cops from your job," he said to Arthur.

"I do; maybe someone I'm familiar with is on duty. I don't think we should take a lot of folks to the stationhouse. We don't want to antagonize the police with a crowd. Scott, I'd like you to go with me."

They went to the police station in Scott's car. The headquarters was in an industrial section of Pacific Grove. Scott pulled into the visitor spot and, while walking to the front door, stepped aside as two officers pulled a handcuffed man through the open door. Once inside, Arthur greeted the sergeant on duty at the front desk.

"Hi, Glen; good to see you."

"No news story today, Arthur, unless you want to do a piece about me," he said, smiling.

"I'm sure that would be interesting to our readers, but we're here about a young man brought in on drug charges; actually, the arrest was for the purchase of marijuana, I suspect, from an undercover officer. His name is Jeff Ronan, and has long hair, nice face."

"The hippie?"

Arthur said, "I was labeled an old timer when I called him that. Apparently, the word is passe. Jeff is a good kid, married, and living in an apartment complex filled with sailors and their families. I live there as well. I'll keep an eye on the kid; my friend here, Lieutenant Oliver, will help me keep him in line."

The desk sergeant frowned. "You're not going to publish an article on the police letting drug users off easy, are you?"

"Of course not. You said *drug user,* so you know he didn't buy to distribute. Can you cut him some slack?"

The desk officer puffed a breath of cigarette-scented breath. "He doesn't have a record, plus the undercover cop is new to the job. There was never an exchange of money or pot. I could book Ronan on intent, but if the case went before a judge, we'd be faulted for not letting them complete the transaction before making the arrest. We haven't put him in the system yet. If I see the kid again, you know what will happen."

"Thank you, Glen; you won't regret it."

"You owe me one, Arthur. Wait here, I'll have him brought out."

Arthur saluted the sergeant, and they sat down to wait for Jeff.

"Why did you tell him I was a lieutenant?"

Arthur explained. "I thought it might improve our position by having a Naval officer involved. I know Glen's son is in the Navy."

Jeff hugged Arthur and Scott. "I don't know what you did to get me out."

Arthur answered, "We told him we'll watch you to ensure this doesn't happen again."

They went back to the apartments. Debbie embraced everyone standing near the pool and cried when she held Jeff. Scott saw Melinda standing near her door.

"How did you guys do it?" someone asked.

"Arthur was the one who got Jeff released. I'm sure Jeff will tell you all about it some other time; he must be exhausted. It's getting late," Scott said aloud.

Melinda approached Scott. "You were calm, knew what you had to do, especially involving Arthur. I told you before you'd make a good officer. I'm proud of you. Will I see you tomorrow?" She kissed him.

~ * ~

A few days later, when Scott was in front of his apartment, he saw Diane on her way back from shopping, carrying two bags, and he rushed to her. Diane handed him the heavier bag as they walked toward her place. At her door, she thanked him.

"I wanted to talk to you, Scott, but not in an open area. I can go to your apartment, but to avoid stares, I'll bring Mariam carrying a cake or some other dessert. You can imagine what I want to discuss; Mariam knows my thoughts. I won't mention it to Melinda and ask that you don't."

At seven, there was a knock on his door, and both women came in; Mariam carrying a cherry pie.

"Store bought," Mariam said, "the best I could do on short notice."

His two neighbors sat on the couch while Scott took the chair.

"I know your relationship with Melinda has been getting serious..."

"Getting serious!" Mariam interrupted, "The girl talks about nothing else."

Diane stared at her friend and continued, "And I'm sure the two of you have discussed all the pitfalls, but I'm worried she'll be hurt when you get orders."

"We have discussed our limited time together; however, neither can walk away from what we have."

"Melinda was a wreck when Teddy died to the point she ate barely enough to survive. Her mental state was far worse... a psychiatrist specializing in grief counseling couldn't help her.

Amazingly, she could do her job, but once home, she stayed in her room, often crying. I'm afraid of her reaction to losing someone else she cares about."

"If I told her we shouldn't continue, what reason would I use? We discussed my leaving for my duty station at length, as well as her return home. I care about her very much and will do what I can to minimize the hurt when I leave. We both will suffer the loss; however, maybe there is a way we can keep our relationship despite the separation. I say this only to you; I won't make promises to her that I might not be able to keep."

"I never doubted you care about her; you are good for her because you are different than Teddy. You've taught my sister that she can care again. Melinda is a positive woman and not, by nature, a cynical person. I wouldn't want her to become one if she loses another relationship, recognizably under different circumstances. I've known women who are disappointed in their relationships; eventually, they question whether love will ever happen another time. Anyway, I appreciate that you've listened to me."

"Diane, I have a kid sister, and if she were in a relationship that would hurt her even if unintended, I would probably talk to the guy in the same way."

On Thursday, Scott left his apartment on the way to the parking lot when he saw Melinda and Diane talking. He started to walk away when he heard Melinda shout, "Hey." He saw her walking fast toward him.

Standing next to him, she said, "You look nice. On a date?"

"No, I'm having dinner at my friends' house. They invite me periodically to ensure I get nourishing food. I told them about the three-women Welcome Wagon at the apartments, but they still insist."

"We still going to the movies on Friday?"

"Yes. I'm not sure why you want to see *An Officer and a Gentleman*. Don't you get enough of the Navy?"

"I'm hoping it inspires someone. See you Friday."

Arriving at the couple's door, Scott was greeted by a quick hug before Julie ran into the kitchen, saying the pot was overboiling. "She doesn't fuss over my meals," Clay said as he yanked out the cork from a wine bottle. She went back into the living room and sat across from Scott.

"You still look good, not malnourished. I don't recall you cooking when you three lived at the other house, so it must be the Welcome Wagon."

"Speaking of the three, have you heard from our other roommate, Mark?"

Clay answered, "He'd sent a gift for our wedding, which included his address. Julie sent him a thank you card with this house number. He's likely at sea by now."

"He had a girlfriend, but they broke up, adding that it was tough maintaining a relationship when you know you'll be gone a lot," Julie added. "Which reminds me, how's Melinda?"

"Great. Things are going well between us. Her sister is not crazy about our involvement for understandable reasons. I know she is looking out for her sister, which, according to Melinda, she's always been there for her."

"You have told her your big secret that you're an officer, haven't you? Sorry, sorry, I know I promised I wouldn't push you on that."

"You didn't think you would get a meal without a lecture, did you?" Clay said.

"As long as we are discussing secrets, have you heard more from your engaged maid of honor, Denise?"

"Considering her deception with you, the term maid of *honor* is not appropriate. She called yesterday; she's doing fine. We don't talk about you or what happened between you. We had a nice conversation about her future wedding. Enough about all that; let's have dinner."

Nine

On Friday, Scott picked up Melinda, and they had a light dinner before the movie. She asked about his time with his friends.

"You go there a lot, it seems, so how was it?"

"Clay and Julie are good friends I've known since I came here; I'd like you to meet them, especially since they ask about you."

"I can cook as well as my partners on the Welcome Wagon, as you call it. Why don't I make dinner for us on Sunday. I can buy the ingredients the day before."

"Will you prepare it at your apartment and bring it over?"

"I'll cook the meal at your apartment, and you can help, especially with the dishes afterward."

In the theater, Melinda looked at Scott periodically while the movie played.

After the showing, they drove back to the apartments, entering a wooded, two-way road before reaching their neighborhood.

"I'm not going to get in trouble with your sister for keeping you out late, am I?" Scott joked.

"No more than you are get yelled at by your instructor for yawning in class."

~ * ~

That Sunday, Melinda arrived at his apartment around five carrying a cardboard box with food to be prepared. Scott took the box from her and placed it on the kitchen table.

"Before you start getting ready, I wanted to talk to you about something related to the dinner with friends." She sat on the couch while he poured wine, handing her a glass as he sat. "I've told you that Clay and Julie are good friends, and Clay was one of two roommates before coming here. I was the best man at their wedding, partnering with Julie's friend, Denise, from her hometown. I spent time with Denise, perhaps too much, because something developed between us. She left shortly after the wedding, which was when I learned she was engaged. I was bothered by the deceit; I haven't spoken to her since then."

"Did you want a relationship with her?" Before he could answer, Melinda added, "But the distance was an obstacle, right?"

"Maybe at first, but not after I learned she was planning to get married. The miles apart would have been an impediment. I know you are comparing that with us, but it's not the same."

"I appreciate you sharing that with me. I'm also glad she lied; otherwise, we wouldn't have been together. Of course, distance will eventually be an obstacle for us."

"Nothing could block me from wanting to be with you."

She kissed him and said, "I'd better get dinner ready. You can help by getting me your pots and pans. You do have them, don't you?"

"Yes; one roommate went aboard a ship, and the newly married friends got plenty as wedding gifts, both leaving everything in the kitchen in the prior house. Plus, some came with the apartment."

They worked together in preparing the chicken dinner and accompanying vegetables, occasionally bumping into each other in the small space.

"This is delicious, Melinda," he said between forkfuls, "Being here is much more enjoyable than at a restaurant," and leaning toward her, "Also, I don't get to kiss the cook there."

When they were finished eating, Scott looked around. "I don't see dessert."

Melinda rose from the table, grabbed his hand, pulling him toward his bedroom. Once inside, she unbuttoned and yanked off his shirt. She started to loosen her blouse until Scott took her hand away to unfasten the buttons. Adeptly, he reached behind her to unzip her mid-thigh skirt, which dropped to the floor as she stepped out of her shoes. Scott removed his pants until they were both in their underwear. Before he continued kissing her, Scott lowered the bedspread and, with his hands on her back, lowered her to the mattress. Facing each other, they kissed hungrily, tongues touching. Scott unclipped her bra and tossed it to the edge of the bed, momentarily staring at her freed breasts. Both paused to remove their sole garments and clung together, their naked flesh joined.

"Scott," she whispered, "this is not my first time, but it is my first with you. I want it to be special."

He reached into the drawer alongside the bed and yanked off the foil covering of a condom. Melinda arched her back and pushed her hands against his back. They moved in a close rhythm; the bed creaked under the frantic motion. Afterward, he watched her as she opened her eyes to look at him. She settled close and kissed him. They stayed motionless for a while.

"This was much better than cake."

"But you've never tasted my latest cake."

"Melinda, please stay the night. I don't want you to leave."

She sat up. "I can't."

"Why not?" he asked as he rose. "Are you concerned with the gossip or worried about your sister's reaction?"

"Neither; I could stay like this for a long time, but I can't get used to spending nights with you, can't develop the routine of being here all the time, being in your bed with you, watching you close your eyes, and waking alongside you. That would soon make it more difficult."

"My leaving for a duty station hangs over everything: our conversations, our decisions, our future. I wish you would stay, but I understand. Just stay a bit longer in bed."

"Does that mean I don't have to do the dishes?"

Scott hugged her. "I'll take care of the kitchen. By the way, you are a great cook but not the neatest. What a minute! Did you seduce me to get out of doing the cleanup?"

Ten

Scott came out of his apartment and saw two women in the pool—a man was sitting on the concrete edge, his head moving with the women's swimming. Recognizing Melinda as one of the women, Scott walked toward where they had gathered. Upon seeing him, Melinda jumped out of the water with the other female following.

"This is Margie Newman and her husband, Louie. She and I have become swimming buddies."

"Pleased to meet you both. Are you the timekeeper, Louie?"

"No, the lifeguard who will apply mouth-to-mouth to either as needed."

"You go near anyone's mouth but mine, you're in big trouble," Margie said.

"Scott, are you playing softball this Sunday?" Louie asked.

"I didn't know anything about it."

Melinda said, "I was tasked with asking you to play and Arthur to referee. The teams are male-female, but husbands and wives can't be on the same side. That also applies to you and me, which tells you how we are viewed. I'm sure you're good at baseball or softball, but I'm not."

"You don't need a glove. There are plenty of extras around, or you can switch with someone on the opposing team," Louie explained.

"Are Ralph and Ingrid going?" Melinda asked about a couple that had moved in recently.

"No," Louie answered. "She told Margie they had plans that day. I think she feels sweating is beneath her, acting like she's a snooty officer's wife."

Scott bit his lower lip.

"I'm going in now," Melinda said as she walked to her apartment.

Scott saw Louie's eyes follow her, focusing on the lower portion of her body.

~ * ~

The sun had dissolved the remnant clouds, clearing the sky to allow the full warmth of the rays to penetrate. Scott picked up Melinda as she came out of the apartment in tight shorts, a t-shirt, and sneakers. He tried not to stare at her braless breasts beneath the cotton but failed.

"Is it that obvious?" she asked, sensing his awkwardness.

"No, no, not at all. I hope you get a hit so you can run the bases."

"Wise guy! I'll be right out." In a few minutes, she came back out, the bouncing contained, to Scott's amusement.

The baseball field was in the nearby park. Bases were slates planted in the hard soil. Lines were painted to mark from home to first base as well as third base to home. The grass was cut low while the base paths were cleared of growth. As expected, Scott and Melinda were assigned to opposing teams. She played right field for a few innings, her inexperience showing when she dropped a soft fly ball hit in her direction. Her final time at bat came in the last inning with a team player on third base, one out, the score tied. Before the game, Scott showed her how to hold the bat. "Watch the ball once it leaves the pitcher's hand. I hear the guy throws underhand hard, nearly straight in, not a lob."

While standing at the plate, she swung at the first pitch, causing the infielder to taunt. "Any easy out," he shouted.

A few guys on her team shook their heads as she swung late at the next pitch, just as the ball struck the catcher's glove. The runner at third dug his heel into the dirt, ready to run if she hit the ball. As the pitcher brought his arm forward to release the ball, Melinda stared at him, suddenly shaking her buttocks, drawing the catcher's eyes with her motion. The ball sailed past the catcher's glove, rolling to the edge of the field while the runner took off, needlessly sliding into the unguarded home plate.

Several players on the field shouted in protest, but Arthur, as home plate umpire, shrugged his shoulders. The game ended with Melinda's team as the winner. Louie, who'd been playing on her team, hugged her and slapped her butt softly. "Good use of assets," he said.

Scott charged toward them, but Melinda shook her head to stop him. She leaned toward Louie. "You ever touch my ass again, I'll kick yours."

~ * ~

Scott and Melinda developed a routine: she'd come to his apartment several times a week, share a meal that was either take out or something she quickly prepared, give him a weekly shopping list, and leave early evening. On weekends, Melinda, despite her earlier reluctance, stayed over on Saturday. Occasionally, they varied from the routine; Scott offered to make dinner once, but the result was a disaster and he had to put up with Melinda's constant giggling at his attempt before he gave up and ordered pizza. At times, she helped him with his studies, chuckling at the unfamiliar words and his attempt at mimicking the intonations. The intimacy increased as well. After a meal or talking on the couch, they went to his bedroom and made love. On Sunday, after waking up together, he joined her in the shower, and the naked proximity led to them falling on the bed, still wet. Scott missed her on the days they weren't together, but Melinda explained she needed to spend time with her sister, "Otherwise, I'd be using their place like a tourist uses a hotel room."

Melinda told Scott she slept better in his bed than the one in her sister's apartment, but Scott was restless at night. When she was facing him in her sleep, he looked at her, her face serene, a half-smile on her lips, and her eyelids occasionally fluttering as if dreaming. When his back was turned, she placed her arm over his back, rested her hand on his chest, her breath on his neck, and slid against him so close he could almost feel her heart beating.

Having her at his apartment also created risks of being discovered. He feared she would open his closet door and see his uniform, especially after she remarked one day, "I have never seen you in uniform. You must zip around the corner to the parking lot and, after class, change at the gym."

"You don't want to see me in uniform; I look like every other sailor in this development."

"Luke taught me about the different markings on a sailor's sleeve: one stripe means seaman recruit, two means seaman apprentice, three is seaman, four is..." She paused, lifting her head. "I wanted to see if you were listening. The next rate is actually a third-class petty officer. Are you impressed?"

"Very much so."

"What are you? I hope the Navy recognizes that you have a college degree. Is your uniform in the closet? I help Diane to pay for my keep, including pressing Luke's uniform once. I could do yours. I'll look for it in the closet."

She rose from the bed until Scott said, "You know how to kill the mood."

"What do you mean?"

"We are in a post-coital calm when you start discussing uniforms."

"Okay, I get your point." She laid back down next to him.

Eleven

Scott avoided any mention of passing time and the dread of receiving orders. However, he sensed she was bothered by the days going by. Once, she took off her watch and threw it on the floor. "I hate watches and calendars." A few times as she pressed against him in bed, he could feel the wetness from where her head lay.

Melinda called on a day they'd not planned to meet, saying she had to talk to him. When he opened the door, he could see the anxiety on her face.

She looked at him and said, "I didn't get my period."

"We were careful about using a condom, but I realize they are not one hundred percent effective. I don't recall a time when we didn't take precautions."

"Once, we had sex after a shower. We got caught up, and I don't recall you reaching into the drawer."

Scott slapped his forehead. "You're right. What should we do now, get married?"

Melinda touched his cheek. "You're sweet, but for now, we need to be sure before we do anything. That gets a bit tricky in terms of logistics. I can subtly ask one of the women for the name of a gynecologist without raising suspicions. If I ask Diane, she'll grill me for a reason and offer to drive me."

"I'll take the day off and go with you."

"Can you do that?"

"I'll arrange it."

The doctor's office was in a plain-front medical building in Monterey; they took the elevator to the third-floor office. They sat together in the crowded waiting room after Melinda confirmed her appointment with the receptionist. Waiting for the nurse to call her into the examination room, she grabbed Scott's hand, tightening and loosening her grip. When her name was called, Melinda nearly pulled him from the seat. Scott looked around the room after she left and saw that he was the only male there. A woman across from him smiled nervously. His thoughts were far away as he pondered the implications a pregnancy would bring, including on his Naval career. He hadn't decided on signing up for another enlistment after the current was completed, but a child would likely discourage him from doing so. Despite the possible changes resulting from a child, he felt calm, and a three-person life had an appeal. He'd barely formed his thoughts when Melinda came out of the physician's space, shaking her head, leaving Scott unsure if she was feeling relief or disappointment. They walked to the car, saying nothing until they were inside, when Melinda spoke. "I'm not pregnant."

"How do you feel about that?"

"My future, our future, is unclear; therefore, my time with you now is my only focus. In all likelihood, I'll think about the pregnancy scare later, all the possibilities and pitfalls that would have occurred."

Scott pulled out and drove to the apartment. "We can go back to the ways things were?"

"Yes, of course," her tone rose, "but if you ever forget to use a condom, I'm cutting you off."

Scott put his hand over his crotch, "Ouch, bad choice of words."

He parked in the rear parking lot, and they walked past his apartment after she said, "I'm exhausted." Stopping in front of her place, she kissed him. "Thank you for going with me."

~ * ~

The next day, while leaving his apartment, he saw Diane carrying two shopping bags and offered to take them for her.

"I got these, but one more is in my open truck on the side lot. This is the second time you've carried my purchases."

He lifted the bag, slammed the trunk, and brought the packages toward her apartment. Diane met him midway, taking one of the bags from his arms.

"Did you two have a disagreement? Melinda has been quiet and moody."

"No, not at all," Scott answered.

"Must be that time."

"I wouldn't know."

~ * ~

On a Friday morning, Scott's phone rang. Groggily, he picked up the receiver and looked at the clock, which showed six-thirty. "Hello."

"Oh my god, I'm so sorry, I forgot the time difference again."

"Lilly, sis?"

"Yes, and I have news but go make yourself breakfast. I'll call you again in an hour. Actually, shouldn't you be getting up for language class anyway?"

"The instructor is sick, and they couldn't get a substitute. Friday's class was canceled. Seems to be a lot going around here."

"Talk to you in an hour."

Sipping his coffee, Scott thought about his sister, remembering the day his parents had brought her into the house. Her eyes stared up at him, uncertain who he was. Communication was a challenge, and his mother pointed toward objects throughout the house and pronounced the English words. In addition, they took her for drives to explain the words for things they saw: trees, cars, bicycles, trash cans, mailman, police officer, children playing on the sidewalk, and many other words. His parents called her Lilly, the translation of her Chinese name, Baiche. In time, she was speaking in full sentences and eliminating the up-and-down pronunciation of her native language. Lilly laughed at her adoptive parents' attempt to learn Chinese. As he told the families assembling at Clay and Julie's pre-wedding party, Scott grew close to his sister, protecting her until he realized she could handle her own problems. She grew from a skinny, reticent kid with forming features and dull dark hair to a beautiful young woman with black hair and flawless skin. Scott hadn't seen her since his month-long visit home before reporting for class.

In an hour, Scott said to himself when the phone rang, "Punctual as always."

"Okay, what's the big news? You know, I could have had company when you called."

"Was I interrupting something? Has this to do with the girl in your apartment complex you told me about?"

"She's a woman, not a girl. She nearly bit my head off when I used that word with her. Anyway, I shouldn't have delayed you telling me your news."

"I will continue, but I like that woman already. Hopefully, I'll get a chance to meet her."

"What do you mean by meet her?"

"If you let me explain, you'll know. I have an interview in San Francisco for a job with a consulting firm that advises U.S. companies dealing with Chinese businesses. I guess my finance major and my fluency in Chinese were factors in their interest. I would get the opportunity to travel to China and other Southeast Asia countries. I'm so grateful to our parents for encouraging me to be knowledgeable about my culture. Remember when Mom took me to visit my relatives there, paying for a trip to my birth land when I became eighteen? The company paid for my travel, hotel, plus the flight cost to see my big brother, if only for a day. On Monday, I'm meeting with the firm's partners. I need you to recommend a place to stay near you when I arrive tomorrow. Sorry for the short notice, but this happened very quickly."

"I'm really happy for you; I have a spare bedroom where you can stay. We can go to dinner after I pick you up at the airport."

"Just not a Chinese restaurant," she said. "Everybody assumes I prefer Asian food. I'd love a juicy hamburger or a thick steak."

"I know a great Mexican restaurant."

"My favorite, too. I miss you, brother. Do you know where you'll be stationed next?"

"No, not yet, but I'm not anxious to know right now."

"There's a story behind that probably connected to the young woman. You can tell me all about it when we meet."

She gave Scott the details of her flights.

Later in the day, Scott called Melinda, but Diane answered the phone and said her sister was napping. "I'll call her on Sunday," he told her.

Lilly's plane was arriving at Monterey Regional Airport at two. Standing in the waiting area near the deplaning, he saw his sister exit and was taken aback by her appearance changes in the months since he had seen her last. Her hair was shoulder length, and she wore sunglasses that framed her eyes and hung on her delicate nose. Her tight dress stopped just above her knees. Men around her glanced at her, ignoring the proximity of the women accompanying them. Scott took the suitcase from her hand and they walked to the parking lot. Taking a roundabout trip to show her some of the local sights, he arrived at the apartment. Dropping her suitcase in the extra room, he went into the kitchen, took a bottle of white wine from the refrigerator, and poured it into two glasses.

"You have a nice place, but you haven't done much with it. Then again, your room at home was somewhat spartan."

"Mom wouldn't use that word to describe where I slept; she used words like pigsty or trash can. Tell me about the job interview."

"I would work with a senior consultant until I developed my own clients in a few years after I became more known in the business community. My primary role would be as an intermediary between American companies who want to do business with Chinese manufacturers. I'd travel often to major cities and occasionally to rural sections of China. I'm very excited about the business opportunities and looking forward to down times when I can look up relatives I haven't seen since I was a little girl. I was young when my mother passed away, but I would like to know more about her. I've seen pictures but don't know what she was like. Subject change: tell me about this woman who's captured your heart."

"You've had a long flight, so why don't you freshen up and change into something more comfortable. I was going to take you to the officers' club at the postgraduate school because they have great steaks, but that was too formal. Mexican is a better choice. Afterward, we'll tour other areas since you have so little time."

"Great, I have jeans and a blouse in my suitcase. Give me about fifteen minutes to get ready. I'm starving; plane food is not the best."

At the restaurant, they were greeted by a petite Hispanic woman who led them to a table. The waitress listed the specials in accented explanations. Scott was surprised when Lilly spoke to the woman in Spanish. Scott gave her his order, and Lilly repeated his preferences as well as her own in Spanish. As soon as the waitress left, Scott leaned forward toward his sister.

"When did you learn to speak Spanish?"

"In college, languages came easier to me than most. I know some French and even a few words in Russian. I figure they might come in handy."

The waitress returned with their beer, and Scott, not to be upstaged by his little sister, offered to thank the woman with more than *gracias* but garbled the words.

"Okay, now I want to hear about this young woman who lives in the apartment complex."

Scott exhaled. "She's the sister of another resident and her husband, who, like most people living there, are in the military attending language school. Melinda is attractive, smart, spunky, and easy to be with. We go out, but with my studies, I have little time during the week, so she comes over, and we spend time together. She even helps me study, although she makes fun of my Chinese."

"You were always good with the language, unlike your Spanish."

"I think she likes to harass me. Actually, she is supportive and patient."

"What will happen to the relationship once you leave and go to your next duty station? You've had girlfriends before, but I can sense in your words and facial expressions that she means a great deal to you."

"That question about our future haunts us, indicating the strength of our relationship. Most people, including Melinda's sister, think it's foolish to start something." Scott explained the death of Melinda's fiancé.

"Your relationship is complicated; however, as you say, if it can continue despite all that, you must have something special together."

After they finished eating, Scott said, "I don't imagine you'll meet her, since you're leaving tomorrow, but if there is a remote chance, I need to tell you something else. I've hidden from the renters at the apartments that I'm an officer, including Melinda. I thought I was doing so for the right reason, but the longer the charade went on, the more difficult it was to admit the truth."

"A lie usually requires more lies to continue," Lilly said.

"A good friend I've made here said something similar."

"When a woman tells you you're wrong, consider her opinion; when two women say you made a mistake, you can be certain you screwed up," Lilly said. "I know she'll be hurt when you do decide to be honest, but I suspect both of you will be hurt if the damage is irreparable by prolonging the reveal."

"When the timing is right, I'll tell her."

"Dear brother, men often use that excuse. One more suggestion before I'm quiet: what if she finds out but not from you?"

They declined dessert, and the waitress she put the bill on the table.

"Let's skip that tour to get back to your apartment. I was up early to make my flight and am tired. I'm so glad I got to see you."

When Lilly went to bed, Scott stayed up in the living room thinking about his involvement with Melinda and the lie he'd been maintaining. Unlike Julie, she had no knowledge of the military culture nor the whole back story, but she echoed Julie's warning. As well as he had begun to know Melinda, he wasn't confident of her reaction if he came clean. He dozed on the couch until he woke with a start and looked at the clock before going to bed.

Scott and his sister rose early and talked while they had breakfast. Afterward, Lilly packed the few things she'd taken from her luggage and went into the bathroom to shower. Scott was still in his bathrobe and shorts when there was a knock at the door.

He was surprised when he saw Melinda standing there. She leaped into his arms, loosening the tie on his bathrobe.

"I'm not contagious," she said gleefully, kissing him. She stepped back slightly when she heard water flowing in the bathroom. "You left the shower on; since you're not wet, I guess you're about to go in. I'm sorry I wasn't a few minutes later," she said, licking her lips.

The shower stopped. Melinda's eyes narrowed, and her eyebrows came closer together. A woman came out of the bathroom in a short cotton robe, her hair dripping. Lilly walked toward her brother. Scott put his arm around his sister, pulling her close.

Melinda looked back and forth between them, one likely naked under a small robe and the other, her boyfriend in his shorts and a falling-off bathrobe.

"Stop teasing her, Scott. You must be Melinda. I'd hug you, but I'd get you wet. I'm his sister, Lilly. Didn't you tell her I would be here?"

"In my defense, I haven't talked to Melinda since you called. I did phone her, but her sister said she was sleeping—I assume because she wasn't feeling well."

Lilly looked at Melinda. "Give me a few minutes to finish getting ready, then we can talk. I told Scott I hoped to meet you. He told me you're beautiful."

After she closed the bathroom door, Melinda smacked Scott on the arm. "That was mean, but I forgive you." She kissed him. "Get dressed so we all can chat."

"Be aware that Lilly has to catch a flight to San Francisco later today."

They spoke in the living room, with Lilly explaining why she was there. Melinda gave her background details, which included specifics of her involvement with Scott.

"Now you need to tell me about Scott when you both were growing up," Melinda said. "Start with your favorite story."

Melinda and Lilly sat on the couch while Scott settled on a chair from the kitchen. Lilly looked at her seatmate. "Have you heard about the Chinese Santa?"

Scott shouted, "Lilly, isn't anything sacred?"

"Oh, come on, brother, it's a good story."

Melinda said, "I really want to hear about Chinese Santa."

"I was still very young and getting used to living in America. Our parents took us to the mall, stopping at Macy's to see Santa Claus. I bawled. I was a Chinese girl sitting on the lap of an old white man with a full beard. I was surrounded by people who looked nothing like me. Needless to say, my parents were dismayed. However, Scott had an Asian classmate, which gave him an idea. His school friend lived a few streets from us, and the family had a routine of celebrating Christmas in which the father dressed as Santa; the kids would go to bed early but sneak down to see Asian Santa putting presents under the tree. Their children were likely aware that the man in the red suit was their father, but they kept the tradition for a while. Our mother went with Scott to talk to the couple, asking if the father would come to our house early Christmas Eve in his Santa suit. He agreed, recommending Lilly go to sleep early because busy Santa could come at any time. As they did at their house, Scott and I went to bed with the arrangement that my brother would wake me to get a peek at Santa. I was elated that there was a Chinese Santa who made the trip to my house for me."

"That's a great story, Scott. Why wouldn't you want her to tell me?"

"There was more to the story," Lilly added. "Maybe that's why. Eventually, I learned about the couple a few streets away, deciding to visit them and meet people from my Chinese culture. When I rang their bell, the mother opened up, and I immediately chatted in my native language. She was puzzled, explaining that they were Filipinos, not Chinese. I was so embarrassed that I ran home. Learning the Santa fib, which I later called it, was Scott's doing, I wouldn't speak to him for a week."

"That's Scott, considerate but sometimes clueless."

"I wish I had more time here," Lilly said as she stood. "We could share more stories about Scott."

"I have an idea; I can drive you to the airport in his car. We'll have plenty of time to share notes."

Both looked at Scott, who was frowning.

His sister said, "That's a great idea. Of course, you can't come along, brother, or how else can we talk about you without you getting defensive."

Melinda said, "That's not his main worry because I once drove his car and got a speeding ticket."

"That must be a great story all its own. Scott, could you carry my suitcase to the car while Melinda and I gossip?"

Lilly called Scott from the airport. "She's delightful; I can see why you care about her. I'm sure she feels the same way about you. I'm a bit irritated at you. I nearly told her how proud I was when you got your commission. Tell her before it's too late. I'll call you from home. Love you."

Melinda stopped by after returning from the airport. Knocking on his door, she said, "I have to go back to the apartment, but I wanted to tell you how wonderful your sister is. In addition, she told me more great stories about you."

Scott grabbed her arm and led her to the couch. "I'm sure Lilly told you stories that put me in a positive light, especially relating to our closeness. Sometimes I was jealous of the attention she got, resulting in acting out, especially in my early teens."

Melinda put her hand on his cheek. "We're at the stage of our relationship where we try to create an appealing image. We get a sense of the total self only through knowing each other for longer. But I'm confident that knowing your full personality, including faults, mistakes, and quirks, my feelings for you won't change. Now, I really have to leave."

Twelve

One late afternoon, Scott and Melinda were seated by the pool when Nick Garcia approached them.

"We're planning a celebration for Les Brightman, leaving next week for his duty station. The party will be at the Anchor bar this Thursday. Why don't you join us? About ten guys are going from here, plus a few from his class."

Melinda asked, "I haven't seen his wife lately."

"She went home, where Les will join her before they head overseas." Looking at Melinda, he said, "That's why it's guys only."

"Is Luke going; if so, I'll ask Diane to help gather the women to go out for a drink, not at the Anchor, of course."

"Can we count you in, Scott?"

Scott hesitated until Melinda encouraged him. "Go ahead; you'll have a good time."

The Anchor lived up to its name with nautical photos and paraphernalia on walls—sea scenes, ships with billowing masts, pirate vessels, and, on one wall, the Navy flag. A sailor's hat was stapled near the door. A few couples sat at the oak tables, but most—largely men—were lined up at the mahogany bar filled with partially empty beer glasses. Judging by the short haircuts, Scott figured most were military, probably taking courses at the language institute. He scanned the crowd to ensure there was no one from his class. The guest of honor was seated on a stool, three beer glasses in front of him, one empty. Scott went to him, offering congratulations. The honoree's eyes were glassy, not recognizing Scott until he realized who was speaking. "Thanks, Scott," he mumbled. One of the men from the apartments said, "He started early." Another sailor, along with two others, including Luke, approached Scott.

"I see you're with Melinda. What are the odds that the only bachelor in the development would get involved with the sole girl?"

Simultaneously, Scott and Luke said, "She's not a girl."

"You got the lecture, too," Luke said. "Why don't you explain."

"Melinda gets mad when you refer to her as a girl, saying she's not twelve, she's a woman."

Another in the group raised his glass. "To the women."

Scott stayed an hour and a half longer, getting up to leave when Luke approached him.

"We'll all be leaving soon. As you probably noticed, our celebrant is pretty far along. I'll get his key to take his car home, but would you drive Les back? Leave him in front of his door, upright or prone. A few of us will get him inside and make coffee."

Tugging at Les's arm, Scott said, "I'm your designated driver, so we need to get going."

"Didn't you have a good time?" Les mumbled as he was half-carried to the car. Whistling at Scott's car, he said, "What a car. How can you afford it on what a petty officer third class gets paid?"

"Can you make it in the seat?"

"So mysterious. You know, some guys think you work for the Navy's investigative branch, maybe checking on us so we don't reveal secrets, not that we have any."

On the way back, Les fell asleep so deeply that Scott couldn't get him out of the front seat. When he entered the apartment area, he saw the others walking in.

"Hey, guys," he said, "I can't lift him from the car; he's dead weight."

Luke and another sailor walked to Scott's car and hoisted Les to his feet, dragging him to his apartment door.

Scott headed to his place, but before he got to the door, he saw Melinda, Diane, and four other women coming from the parking lot. Stopping in front of Melinda while the others left for their apartments, he asked: "Have fun?"

She kissed him and asked him the same question. "Did you? We saw you guys yanking Les from your car. You're never getting me inside if he got sick on the seat."

Melinda went to Scott's apartment. She said, "Lilly loves you. That shouldn't be surprising, but your relationship is very special, especially considering there is no blood tie. She did tell me cute stories about you, but more importantly, I got to learn more about you from someone who had a front-row seat."

Scott said, "I did help her with the language in the early years; however, she was my sounding board in my teen years, especially about girls. I admired her, and still do. Going from one culture, from one family to another, was difficult for her, but she never rebelled, was never unappreciative of my parents' support."

~ * ~

The next day, she came to his apartment with a photo album, opening the pages with half the cover in her lap and the other in his. Scott looked at a picture, then at Melinda to see the resemblance. He chuckled at a photo of Melinda in pigtails and a gingham dress. He put his finger on a print of her in her mid-teens.

"You'll have beautiful children," he said.

"Not if they look like you. I didn't mean to assume..."

"We almost found out, didn't we?"

"Scott, I was glad to learn I wasn't pregnant, but there was a part of me that wondered. Let's change the subject; we shouldn't be talking about this."

"Okay, we can talk about something else, but the thought of marrying you and having a child didn't scare me."

They switched to lighter subjects like sharing embarrassing moments from their past.

~ * ~

Scott was running late one morning; hurrying out of his apartment in uniform, so he didn't see Arthur coming out of his.

"Scott," Arthur called, startling Scott.

"I don't have time to explain, so can I stop by your place after class?"

At the end of lessons, he went to the gym, changing without exercising. He knocked on Arthur's door, entering as soon as his neighbor opened. Arthur had a quizzical look even though, as he explained, he had figured out what Scott was doing.

"You were in the military, so you know about the separation between officers and enlisted. I'm neither defending nor opposing the requirement," Scott said. "The bottom line, however, is that it's ingrained. I was concerned that the enlisted in the development would avoid me because of my rank. As time went on, I felt justified because I got to know the guys, which I believe will help me be a better officer once I leave here for a duty station.

My prior tour was in Washington, where I dealt more with other officers or independent contractors. Since I've been in the apartments, I've selfishly enjoyed being one of the guys. I'd likely not have met Melinda or enjoyed the kind of relationship we have."

"Scott, I would be out of place commenting on what you described, but I've seen you with Melinda; you two belong together. It's not because of the newness. I've not been in this complex very long, but it's a great place to observe marriage interaction. I look at some spouses and question whether they will make it through the difficulties and separations, while others, like Luke and Diane, are destined to stay together regardless of the challenges. The problem with being an old man is that I feel paternal, as I do for you and Melinda. Do what you can to stay with her; she's a rare young woman."

"Thank you, Arthur. For now, I appreciate you keeping my secret. By the way, did you suspect when you told the police officer that I'm a lieutenant?"

Arthur nodded. "I sensed you acted differently than most here. I'm a reporter with lots of experience measuring people. The ruse was also necessary to strengthen our position to get Jeff released, as I said."

On Friday night, Melinda stayed overnight at his place. Scott was restless throughout the night. Part of his sleeplessness was due to the need to feel her shift, put her arm over his shoulder, and slide so close that he could feel her breathing. The other cause of his unsettledness was Arthur's comment about Melinda—he was right: they belonged together; he couldn't lose her. Scott woke first, showered and wearing boxers, lathered his face to shave. He kept the door open to release the steam and clear the fogged mirror when Melinda walked in.

"What are you doing?" she asked.

"Trying to shave with this clouded mirror."

"Do you trust me?" she asked.

"Of course," he answered, tilting his head to one side.

Melinda took the razor from his hand while turning his face.

"Have you ever done this before?" Scott asked.

"On my legs; does that count?"

She gently moved the blade down from the edge of his short sideburns, repeating the process on the other side of his face. Lifting his head, she stroked his chin, his neck, under his nose, and around his mouth, periodically rinsing the shaver. She kissed his bare cheek, sniffing at the remnant scent of his shaving cream.

"You do trust me," Melinda said, smiling. "No wounds."

She came back that evening but didn't stay long. When he walked her to her apartment, they saw Diane standing next to a woman Scott didn't know, but guessed she was the wife of a sailor attending language school. Scott told Melinda, "Your sister knows many of the couples here."

"She does, mostly the wives. They ask her for advice because she's been in the Navy longer than most. Many wives here are nineteen or twenty, worried about their lives after language school, with some questioning being married to a sailor who is likely going to sea for long periods. One wife sought my advice, probably because she thinks Diane's skill of discernment is inherited."

"I can understand why someone would go to you—as you said, they are barely out of their teens, and you are an intelligent college graduate. Also, I recall you working in human resources."

"I'm smart, while Diane is wise."

"What did the young woman want to talk to you about?"

"She was really looking for me to talk her out of thoughts of a divorce."

"What did you say?"

"Patty has known her husband since their pre-teen years. I could only explain the experience of losing someone who's been a part of your life for a long time. If she leaves him, he could be out of life forever, as Teddy is mine."

"Do you think about him often? I know you asked not to discuss him."

"Less since you. I don't make comparisons because that would be unfair to you and his memory. I care for you for who you are, not because you have the characteristics or features of someone I once loved. If he were alive, I wouldn't be with you, but his death can't prevent me from eventually loving someone else, loving you if that happens. I cherish the memories of Teddy, but I can't hold memories, and I can't hope for a future with memories. You are real, someone I can hold, someone I could really care about."

"You had a long time to develop those feelings for him, but you and I have no history. How can you be sure of your feelings for me?"

"I said I wouldn't make comparisons, but that's what you're doing. Of course, I knew him well; you and I met recently. I never expected Teddy would do something out of character, something that would hurt me, and I'm confident you won't either. I love surprises, but there has to be certainty in a relationship. That may seem an odd statement considering our unclear future, but I believe you wouldn't leave me if you had a choice."

~ * ~

They were together at his apartment on a Wednesday afternoon after class. Melinda was sitting with Scott on his couch when he said, "I've made plans for the weekend; we're going to Big Sur, staying overnight in a place overlooking the ocean from a height—very romantic."

He picked her up at her apartment on Saturday and carried their suitcases to his car. Highway One dipped south into Carmel Valley, passing the Carmel Mission, stretches of fenced lands with horses nibbling on the verdant grass, then climbing along a borderless road with precipitous drops into the white-foamed ocean. Melinda looked out her window at the closeness of the sea and shuddered. Scott exited the highway and drove a winding road to a hotel at the top of a cliff, the green slope ending at a small stretch of sand.

"Scott, this is beautiful. How can you afford a room here? I never asked, but do you come from a wealthy family?"

"Do you think I'd be staying at our apartments if I was rich? I want to impress you. As I mentioned once before, I'll have plenty of time to save with little options to spend aboard a ship."

"Are you certain you will be on a ship?"

The likelihood is high, but let's not talk about that."

They checked in at the circular wooden desk in the front section of the building. The receptionist handed Scott the room key, but Melinda snatched it before he reached it. The paneled room had a large window overlooking the ocean, and the puffed clouds settled above the waves. A fireplace heated the room; the square bed on an oak base occupied much of the main space. A couch was against the near wall, and two squares of raw wood were used as end tables. Outside, the circular deck had a glass fence, two reclining chairs, and an extended umbrella.

Melinda spun around in the center of the room. Pointing to the section alongside the bathroom, she said, "They have a bar and small refrigerator. I bet there are bottles of wine inside. No TV."

"You want to watch television with that view?"

She put her arms around his neck, "No, I don't. Do they have a restaurant here? I'm starving."

They ate in the dining room, which had glass walls similar to the guest rooms, offering a panoramic view. Wood beams held up the oak roof. The wood motif extended to the table tops and chair backings. They sat at a place near the west-facing glass. A waiter took their drink orders and disappeared behind the round bar, soon carrying a bottle of Chardonnay in a chilling container and two glasses embossed with the hotel name. After they ordered their meal, Melinda sat back, holding her wine glass.

"This is wonderful. I feel so pampered, almost aristocratic. I could get used to this."

"After this, we get to enjoy the best luxury of the hotel—the large hot tub just outside our room."

"You didn't tell me to bring a bathing suit."

"You don't need one. Big Sur was where hippies came to bathe nude in the ocean or stay at communes in the area that hotels now occupy. I'm sure the hotel retains tradition, plus no one will be in the heated water. If they are, I don't think they'll be suited."

Melinda checked on the bathroom and found two robes. Undressing, she looked into the mirror and said, "Not bad." Clothed in a robe, she handed the other robe to Scott. "We can be naked in the water, but not before, just in case."

Scott stripped; both went outside and into the hot tub, leaving their robes on a chair.

"You're beautiful," he told her, looking at her partially submerged body.

Paddling toward him, Melinda stopped so close that the water between them was nearly squeezed out. They kissed and held tightly to each other, ignoring the few drops of rain that fell from errant clouds. The moon was in the clear section of the sky and spotlighted their combined forms in the water.

"I will never forget this night. I love you," Melinda said.

"I love you, too. Let's go inside."

They left the robes on the chair, hastening to the room, leaving wet prints on the floor until their feet were on the bed. The fireplace released waves of warm air. Scott got up from the bed to turn out the lights so the only illumination came from the night sky and the glow of the fireplace. They made love slowly, savoring every movement, heightening the shared passion with their hands until he rolled gently on her. The rhythm of their motions brought them to fulfillment; breathing heavily, they lay flat.

"Did I tell you I love you, Mr. Oliver?" she said.

"Yes, and I said I love you, Ms. Jenkins."

"I don't ever want to leave here, just stay with you, like this, where nothing else exists, nothing will separate us, time is frozen," Melinda said.

"I wish that could be, too."

Part Two

Thirteen

Melinda came to Scott's apartment most nights, sometimes bringing leftovers; at other times, he would pick up takeout. Melinda would also feel guilty about her little time with Diane and Luke. They were asleep by the time she left Scott's apartment on weekday nights.

Scott and Melinda would sit on the couch, she leaning into him while they watched television. He would put his face into her hair, taking in the aroma of her shampoo mixed with the faded odor of her mild perfume. On Friday and Saturday, she slept over, wearing only his Navy t-shirt. They made breakfast together in the morning, parting briefly while she went back to change. Scott deflected any discussion of her staying over during the week, even randomly, using the pretext of needing to get up early to prepare for class—the real reason being to avoid being seen in uniform.

With such time together, they learned a great deal about each other but continued to avoid discussing their relationship status after he received orders. Scott was tempted to come clean about his rank but delayed, especially when lost in her nearness. Melinda was, he recognized, demonstrative in her actions more than in her words, holding his hand when they walked, touching his face, and randomly hugging him, even in public places. In bed, she told Scott repeatedly that she loved him, and he said he loved her.

"All I have is weeks," she said one evening. "Everything says I shouldn't love you, but I do; that makes it so right."

They went out on the weekend, going to movies or dinner, even to the mall where Scott would critique what Melinda was considering for purchase, although he conveyed a preference for her choice of short skirts and tight tops with a lascivious expression on his face. He thought of the sheer nightgown that Julie had embarrassed him with; he bought it for Melinda.

On a Monday afternoon after class, Scott was waiting for Melinda to arrive when a knock came on the door. He barely opened it to see her reach for his hand and pull him out of the apartment.

"Drive me to the drugstore," she said. "Diane has the car, and you won't let me drive yours."

"Why do you need to go to a pharmacy so urgently; are you sick?' He stopped suddenly. "You're not—"

"Of course not. I'm fine, come on."

She yanked him to the drug store's dental care aisle, scanned the rows of toothbrushes, selected one, and hurried to the cashier section. In the parking lot, Scott planted his feet.

"I'm not going anywhere until you tell me what's going on."

"Be patient. I'll show you at your apartment."

Once inside, Melinda went into the bathroom with Scott following. Opening the toothbrush packing, she placed it in a vacant hole in a holder cemented into the wall.

"Now, when you brush your teeth at night when I'm not staying over, you'll think of me."

He kissed her. "I don't need a toothbrush to remind me that I miss you," adding, "But it will help with morning breath when you stay over."

Scott ran toward the living room on his way out the front door until she tackled him before he could make it. They fell on the couch, laughing.

Later, she asked Scott if he was attending the party on Saturday night.

"Three couples are leaving next week. Having completed their language course, the husbands received orders. All three were helpful in organizing parties for others who have left, so they deserve a good sendoff. I know you don't always want to go to these activities, but I'll be there," she added. Her voice suddenly dimmed. "I'm scared. They had only two weeks after they received their assignment."

"It may be different for me. I'll go to the party, but I'd rather spend the time with just you. Everyone in this complex seems to be looking at us when we're together. If I talk to anyone on whatever subject, they invariably ask about us. One woman asked if we were getting married before I had to leave."

"We could try to fool them by avoiding each other, acting like we've had an argument."

"Then you go to my apartment, which contradicts that."

"Or they could think we were going to have make-up sex."

~ * ~

Scott left his apartment late on the night of the event, and most residents were already assembled. Tables were set up for chips, pretzels, dips, along with mounds of cooked hot dogs. As typically arranged, another table was used solely for beer, and overflowing garbage bins were filled with empty cans. Looking to his left, he stopped so quickly he nearly tripped. He saw a face he recognized and panicked. Approaching a couple he barely knew, he tried to draw them into a conversation, but they were puzzled. Scott saw Melinda coming out of her apartment, but before he could reach her, he was stopped by someone calling his name. He saw a resident, Seth Howser, approaching with another man alongside him. Scott's face went white.

"I met one of your classmates last night, so I invited him to the party. He's alone after his wife went home to visit her parents."

Scott recognized Alex Bristol from his class. Alex approached Scott with his hand extended.

"Yes, he is in my class," Scott said. He shook his head slightly, gripping Bristol's hand tightly in a vain effort to warn the sailor not to give him away.

"It's good to see you, sir."

Scott closed his eyes and lowered his head.

Seth took a step back. "Sir? Did you call him that?"

Bristol, whose face was red, didn't answer at first. "He always seems to take charge in the class. We call him that to joke that he's acting like an officer."

Seth said, "Sorry, Alex, but you don't sound credible." Looking at Scott, rephrasing the sentence slightly, Seth said, "Why is he calling you sir? Only officers are addressed that way by enlisted."

Scott hesitated. Seth called out to several of the men nearby, including Luke. "You may want to hear this explanation as to what Scott is hiding." The men stood behind Seth, staring at Scott. The noise lessened as other sailors and a few women came closer.

Alex Bristol spoke before anyone else. "I'm sorry, Lieutenant. I didn't know."

"Lieutenant?" Is that true, Scott?" Luke said, pushing through to get closer.

"Yes... I'm a lieutenant j.g."

Scott looked around at the growing crowd encircling him, their faces mixing curiosity, confusion, and anger. As he scanned, he looked for Melinda but didn't see her; instead, he caught a glimpse of her door closing.

"I'll explain, but now is not the time."

Bristol said, "I should leave since I caused this."

"No, don't go; *you're* one of us," Seth countered.

"But it is best that *I* leave," Scott said. He could feel the sharp stares on his back.

Later, Scott called Melinda, but Diane picked up and told him she didn't want to speak to him. Over the next few days, when he encountered others from the apartment complex, they largely ignored him; the only male willing to acknowledge him was Jeff, since he wasn't military. Scott didn't go to the gym after class, walking to his apartment in uniform. The following week after the unplanned reveal, he saw six male residents sitting on chairs by the pool. As he approached them, he heard Luke, who was in the group, shout, "Attention on deck," the usual command to enlisted to stand when an officer arrives. Scott knew it was a mocking gesture.

"That's not necessary," he said, masking his annoyance. "I wanted to apologize again for my deception."

One of the men raised his voice. "Why, Lieutenant? We don't understand. Were you slumming to see how the other half lived?"

Luke added, "Most of these men came out of boot camp or another training site, not from assignment to a ship or station. I know from experience that officers have staterooms aboard ships while we enlisted are stacked in bunks; we eat in the general mess at prescribed times while officers dine separately and can get a meal anytime. Our families live in enlisted housing in duty stations, but officers live in larger, separate homes. We initiate a salute and, most importantly, are discouraged from mixing socially, which includes the interaction between officers' spouses and enlisteds' wives. Officers are courteous, but we all go our separate ways once the pleasantries are done. I don't understand why you came here."

Scott replied, "At first, I reasoned that displaying my rank through my uniform would make all of you uncomfortable, knowing the traditional relationship between officers and enlisted. However, I got to know so many of you and enjoyed being with you, not as an officer, but simply as one of the guys. It was nice being Scott to all of you, not lieutenant. As time passed, it got more difficult to undo the original lie; I kept telling myself I'd do it soon. I wasn't *slumming* or acting out of curiosity."

"Does Melinda know?" Luke asked.

Scott shook his head. Looking at Luke, he said, "I deceived her as well, telling myself there was time to reveal, but as you saw, things didn't go as I'd hoped. I don't have much time left to convince you all that I'm sorry and to win your respect, not as an officer but as someone who had become a friend."

"There has been talk about you and what you've done to betray us, so I'm not convinced that everyone here will be forgiving. Many wives are angry; their upset is not based on rank."

Rich Reynolds, a recent arrival to the apartments, said. "We may not admit it, but we're scared of what's next after language school, most even studying for assignments in dangerous places in the world. We see this as a time to enjoy the comradery of others who understand the challenges of learning a new, unfamiliar language and what lies beyond. We're upset to find that one of the men we considered as an equal is not. On ships or duty stations, we do the work but are not part of the decisions as to what or how we do our jobs; that's the role of officers. We have to trust that they make the right decisions. To be honest, we wouldn't be confident in an officer who lies."

Scott realized the most disturbing aspect of their words was that they were correct. If he couldn't convince them to forgive him, what chance would he have with Melinda, who likely felt the most betrayed?

Scott had trouble sleeping as their words played through his mind. The only relief the exposure brought was the freedom from being watchful for mistakes, from being seen when he left in the morning in uniform, from meeting a sailor from the apartments at the gym, or in some unexpected, unavoidable way like what happened with Bristol. He was proud of being a commissioned officer, but that achievement was also the cause of his current distress. Scott knew that, in time, their fury wouldn't matter when they would all go their separate ways, forming opinions of officers based on men and women they encountered at their assigned sites. Only Melinda would remain the loss that would not be diminished by time if he couldn't gain her forgiveness.

~ * ~

Scott, still in uniform, parked in the side lot after class instead of the rear area, hoping he'd see Melinda while he walked to his apartment. Instead, he noticed Diane opening the door to her car. He called to her, stopping her from holding the car door. Jogging to her, he asked if they could talk.

"I'm going to the commissary at Fort Ord and have to be back to make dinner, so if you want to talk, go with me."

"Okay. I need some things myself." He got into her car.

On the drive, she said, "I guess you want to discuss Melinda."

"I really miss her, Diane. I need to explain but mostly apologize."

"She doesn't understand why, nor do any of us."

Scott offered the same reasons he'd provided to the group at the pool while she listened without interruption.

"Scott, before I married Luke, I worked for a corporation, and we bitched about our boss, whose only fault was being a boss. After our wedding, I went with my husband to his first duty station. I heard other enlisted complain about officers, my point being that it's common to gripe about leaders whom we respect even if we don't admit it. I believe you would have been accepted despite the officer's bars on your uniform once they knew you. This is the third tour for Luke and me, so we know what military life is like, but most in the apartments have come from boot camp or preliminary training, so they don't understand the whole officer-enlisted thing. Since you arrived, you've been invited to activities and welcomed into homes. We brought you food partly because we thought you probably struggled financially as we all do."

"Is there anything I can do to be accepted again?"

"You need to understand that the apartments are a refuge for all of us, a place where we share the same hopes and fears, where we live among equals. Melinda mentioned you knew your language well before you arrived here. There are others in our group who struggle. You may have met the Lockwoods; they left quietly last week because he failed his course. Melinda complained that couples at the apartment were gossipy and nosy about your relationship, but I tried to explain that she was wrong. People cared about her, were glad to see her meet someone, and knew she was hurt by being blindsided. They liked you, too, which made the deception more upsetting."

"Is Luke also pissed at me... what about you?"

"You came to our house for dinner. Luke considered you one of his best friends in the apartments. I know you love my sister and have been good to her."

"I am sorry that you and Luke are upset with me and, of course, distraught over Melinda's rejection."

"What do you expect me to do, convince her to go back with you?"

"No. I wouldn't put you in that position; besides, Melinda will make up her own mind."

"She was hurt. Melinda is vulnerable; I've told you that often enough. That vulnerability, however, can become a defense mechanism and prevent a reconciliation."

"She can be a strong woman, rarely letting me get away with anything, but at times, I could sense her vulnerability, especially when she talked about her former boyfriend."

"You really do know my sister, but this situation is different from her relationship with Teddy beyond the obvious. Melinda blamed herself for causing Teddy to speed, but there was no clear proof that he was going at a high speed when the other vehicle hit him—the police admitted that. Deep down, she knew no one was at fault. But you are at fault for what's happened now. That may make it hard to forgive. She's my sister, and I hate seeing her in pain again."

Scott said, "I have a sister, Lilly, who struggled with acceptance in a new culture. She suffered from depression at the time, and I would have done anything to help her get over it, including punching her taunters."

"Obviously, you love your sister; you can understand how I worry about mine."

Diane showed her military ID when they reached the entrance gate to Fort Ord. The soldier on duty nodded. Looking across at Scott, he suddenly stiffened to salute. Scott returned the acknowledgment with one eye glancing at Diane.

After they'd passed the main gate, she said, "Now I understand why you wouldn't go with us to the commissary. If you were in front of us, we would have seen the salute, or if you were behind us, we might have seen the exchange through the rearview. If you were in the car with us, the cat would have definitely been out of the bag. What you had to go through to keep up the—" She didn't finish the sentence.

The commissary was a large structure with an extensive, largely filled parking lot. When Scott commented on the number of cars, Diane said, "Payday for enlisted." He wasn't sure if that was simply an explanation or a dig. Each grabbed a cart from the rack before going inside the cavernous building.

"I likely have more to get than you do, so we'll split up here; you can either look for me or meet me at the cashier."

About fifteen minutes later, Scott had completed his purchases and looked for Diane, finding her in the chilled section of the store picking up meat packages. She looked into his cart and shook her head.

"Chocolate flavored cereal does not qualify as a healthy breakfast." She walked a short distance to the cereal aisle, selected a whole grain brand, and dumped it into his cart. She pointed toward the section where they stored the vegetables and fruit; the gesture was a command, not a direction. Diane picked out bananas and salad, crossing the aisle to locate canned vegetables. "I'm sure you wouldn't know how to prepare raw spinach, corn peas, or anything not pre-packaged. My sister hasn't changed your dining habits."

"I have to learn to cook since I won't be getting care packages periodically," he said with a sly grin.

"Maybe you will after I talk to Mariam, but don't expect Melinda to show up."

"Wait just a minute. Let me see your shopping list," Scott said. After she handed it to him, her cheeks flushed. "I got a glimpse earlier, but now I know you sort your items by aisle."

"You've never shopped with Melinda. If I selected food the way she does, up and down the aisle, no order, filling the cart would take twice as long. I suspect you do as well. You two are a lot alike."

They walked to the cashier, with Scott completing his purchases quicker, waiting near the automatic doors for her to finish. On the drive back to the apartments, Scott looked at Diane at times. He had seen her often and had been to her apartment for dinner but was so focused on Melinda he didn't really recognize the strong resemblance. Both were pretty women, Diane being taller by about two inches, with darker, longer hair and a rounder face with the same striking green eyes, although covered by wire-framed glasses. Their voices were similar, but he could tell the difference when he called. He expected a more negative reaction from Diane, having observed her as the protective sibling. At times, she would look at him when invited to dinner in her place, trying to understand his feelings toward her sister with a stare that was a mix of curiosity and caution. He was pleased she was willing to forgive his deception, at least partially. He decided to ask.

"I thought you, more than anyone else, would be the angriest with me, not want to see or talk to me, yet you've been kind."

"I know you didn't do this to hurt Melinda, even though I wish you hadn't started this mess. Maybe you two will get back together, so I don't want to be an obstacle by holding a grudge, which my sister would immediately detect. Luke may be a challenge to get to the same point. You're a good guy who made a bad mistake, which may cost you much more than my friendship."

Diane removed her shopping list in the apartment parking lot and tore an unused section from the bottom. "With time running out, you may not resolve the separation. You could get orders soon, or she could decide to go home soon, leaving no way for you and Melinda to communicate. Here's my parents' address and phone number," she said while she wrote. "Melinda will be living there initially, although she'll want her own place eventually. Even so, you can contact her through my folks if she does move out."

Scott offered to help her with the packages, but she declined. "I'll take two in, and Luke will get the rest. When I see her, I'll mention to Melinda that we were both at the commissary, not telling her what we've discussed if she asks, which I hope she does, maybe not right away, but eventually. I'll wait a few minutes until you bring your stuff in, so you and Luke don't bump into each other," Diane said.

~ * ~

A few days later, Scott saw Diane briefly, but she never mentioned Melinda.

Clay called that evening to, as he said, 'catch up,' and Scott told him how his ruse had been revealed.

"Julie is shopping, but she'll want to hear the whole story. Come for dinner tomorrow, and you can give us both a rundown."

Scott arrived at their house at six. Julie greeted him at the door and hugged him tightly, after which she punched his arm.

Scott teased. "I knew what your reaction would be: support followed by chastisement."

"That's nothing compared to the sympathy and yelling that will follow. Right now, I'm just sorry for you, expecting that your relationship with Melinda has been impacted. Let's have a glass of wine since the meal will take about a half hour to cook."

Clay came out of the kitchen with three partially filled glasses.

After they were seated in the living room, Scott explained.

"A sailor in my class was invited to a party in the apartments, and when he saw me, he called me 'sir,' which was overheard. Things went downhill quickly before I decided to leave, thinking it was best to let matters settle before trying to explain. A few days later, I spoke to some of the apartment residents, and they aired their resentment while I offered my excuse, which didn't sway them. They were angry but I believe they were also disappointed in me, which hurt the most. They were upset over the deception but surprised that, as an officer, I would go to the lengths I did to hide my rank. One man accused me of 'slumming.' Of course, the whole officer-enlisted dynamic entered into it. Now, I wear my uniform openly, uncertain if seeing me in uniform will enflame their ire or illustrate that I would be open from then on. I watch to see if some men and women are easing their upset, but so far, I'm still a pariah."

"What about Melinda—how did she react? Have you talked to her? "Julie asked.

"No, I haven't. When I call, she won't talk to me. I think her sister, Diane, pities me but knows Melinda will make her own decisions regarding our relationship. Diane warned me that Melinda is still hurting from the death of her fiancé, leaving her vulnerable. I've had time to think and realize my reasons for creating the deceit seem so shallow, not only of the initial lie but of all the ways I came up with to continue the deception, especially with her. I was putting off telling her, afraid of the harm to our relationship, but I didn't consider how hurt she would be and the damage to someone still weakened by the death of someone she loved. I was selfish, only focusing on *my* loss. If I'd been honest with her early on, I could have dealt with the wrath of the whole apartment group, knowing at least my relationship with her was intact. If I'd told her earlier, however, she could have been equally a target of the residents' anger. The first question I got was: did she know. The question came from her brother-in-law, Luke. Okay," he said, looking at Clay and Julie, "go ahead and say *I told you so.*"

Julie walked to Scott's chair and put her arms around his shoulders. "I'm not going to blame you or make you feel worse. I suspect you've been hard enough on yourself that you don't need me to add to it."

"Is there any hope she'll come around?" Clay asked.

"I don't know, plus time is running out. I'll never see her again if I leave here before we resolve this. My sister had called me and asked me if Melinda was the one, but I couldn't answer because I didn't know what that meant or what I should be feeling. All I know is that I've never felt this way about another girl or woman, and can't picture my life without her. Did you two feel that way about each other at first?"

The married couple looked at each other before chortling in near unison. "Absolutely not."

Julie explained. "We didn't like each other; I thought Clay was a snob."

"I considered her flighty."

Julie continued. "We soon realized our first impressions were hasty, and the attraction grew. Like you, we didn't have a lot of time to understand each other fully, but we were certain. Not quite love at first, but pretty close to it. Don't give up if you feel part of what we felt."

Clay said, "If you feel the relationship will end once you leave for your duty station, is it fair to restart only to disappoint in a short time, especially if she is, as you mentioned, vulnerable?"

"She is vulnerable, but not weak. Melinda once said she knew I didn't want the relationship to end, but the Navy could accomplish it for us if we don't talk before I report to my duty station."

"I wish I could talk to her, even though I never met her," Julie said.

"What would you say to her?" Scott asked.

"I would tell her you're a good guy who loves you, made a big mistake, got caught up in an effort to fit in."

"Thanks, but this is not the time to make a plea on my behalf, especially now. I wish you had met her; I promise you will if we get through this."

"You can come here after class from now on if you'd like," Julie offered.

"You two are just married; do you really want me hanging around all the time? I'm not going to change my routine except that I won't hide my uniform anymore; I won't hide who I am."

Clay asked, "Did no one ever figure out previously?"

"No, except for my neighbor, Arthur, no one questioned me or looked quizzically as if they were trying to figure out something about me. I never denied having a college degree, but, as I mentioned to Melinda, enlisted have degrees. One sailor in my class and two in the apartments have degrees. Melinda repeatedly encouraged me to apply to OCS, so obviously, she didn't suspect."

Over the following days, Scott waited for Melinda to call, having tried to reach her without success. With each day passing, his hope of hearing from her diminished. He called about his orders and was told again that they were forthcoming. At night, he slept poorly, especially on the weekend, missing her closeness and making love with her. One night, when he got a call from his sister, Lilly, he held back from telling her about Melinda, unwilling to interrupt her good news about the offer she'd received from the California company. When she asked about Melinda, he hesitated, raising her suspicion.

"We're not seeing each other," he offered as a brief description, knowing Lilly wouldn't leave it at that.

"What happened?"

Scott explained all that had occurred, adding his sense that he'd never see her again. He expected Lilly would scold him. She didn't.

"I'm sorry, brother. But I'm upset with her since she won't talk to you, give you a chance to explain."

"I can explain but not explain away. There was no excuse to keep my deception from her. She was with me constantly, slept in my bed, said she loved me."

"While she didn't tell me her feelings about you, I knew she loved you."

"I love her. The situation is so convoluted, with little time to resolve it. Anyway, I'm very glad to hear about the job. By the way, I never mentioned Melinda to Mom and Dad..."

"I did. They were pleased to hear you were involved in a serious relationship. We were all glad for you. You dated, but I can't recall anyone you brought home, anyone special in your life. If the relationship with Melinda doesn't work out, don't let it deter you from finding love."

"You are such a romantic. I love you, sis."

Fourteen

Scott settled on the couch, opening a textbook, when there was a loud banging on the door. Expecting that something was very wrong, he was taken aback to see Melinda, tears flying from her eyes as she shook her head.

"How could—" She could barely speak; the words were stuck in her throat.

"Please sit so we can talk."

"I can't because if I'm near you, I'll want to hold you or slap you. I don't want to do either."

"I would welcome the embrace and deserve the slap, so either is okay."

They sat on the couch, Melinda moving as far from him as possible.

"I don't know why I came here; I don't know what I want from you, not an apology, not an explanation. I opened the apartment window and heard your excuses to the men."

"Melinda, I was not excusing what I did; I was explaining. There is no excuse."

"All the lies. I encouraged you to become an officer, but you already are. I bet you had a good laugh about that. I shared my feelings with you about so much of my history. You were holding back all the time, not telling me about a major segment of your life. For god's sake, I told you I love you. We made love; I slept in your bed while this huge lie hung over our heads. People here think you must have shared your deception with me. I'm being snubbed by some people who once greeted me, but I don't care what they think. I don't understand why you wouldn't tell me, even if you kept it from everyone else. How could I ever trust you if you wouldn't trust me? Did you think I'd tell Diane, that I couldn't keep your secret, even though I disagreed with the idea?"

"I can't justify why I kept you in the dark except I was afraid I'd lose you. The irony is that the longer I kept it from you, the longer I was convinced you'd leave me once you knew, or I wouldn't have enough time to secure your forgiveness. Regardless of my reason for maintaining the lie with everyone in these apartments, I should have known that keeping this farce from you was wrong. I would have told you before one of us left here; I realize that matters little now. I don't want to lose you, Melinda."

"Scott, remember you told me about that bridesmaid who didn't tell you she was engaged?"

"Denise, yes."

"She hurt you because you cared about her; I bet you even hoped to continue seeing her somehow."

"Where is this leading?"

"What was your reaction when you found out she deceived you?"

"I never wanted to see or talk to her again."

"You didn't want to hear her explanation, even though she didn't lie to you, she just didn't tell you the truth."

"No, I didn't."

"You were upset because you couldn't understand why she betrayed you. Then you can understand why I don't want to hear you or see you again." She stood. "Goodbye, Scott."

~ * ~

He went into a tailspin with little interest in studying; his appetite disintegrated, and sleep was impossible. All he could think about was the brief, one-sided confrontation followed by the image of Melinda running out the door, her sobs audible. His feelings ran from regret for what he'd caused to anger at not being allowed to talk. Every place in his apartment was a reminder: the couch, the table, the bathroom, and the bed. He restarted his routine as an escape, going to the gym as before, lengthening the time on the equipment until his muscles were so sore he had to stop for a day. Julie called every few days, extending an offer of dinner, but he declined. After two weeks without seeing Melinda, he reconciled himself that the relationship was over when there was a knock at the door, and he was surprised to see Diane and Mariam with trays of food.

"Come in, please. I never expected the food visits to continue."

Mariam looked at him. "This was Diane's idea; we had to pass a gauntlet of disapproving eyes, especially from our spouses. I added the spices to the chicken and considered arsenic as a condiment."

The women place the tin trays on the kitchen table.

"I asked Mariam to come with me, but then leave so I can talk to you."

As if cued, Mariam left while Diane pulled out a chair at the table,

"Scott, I've not asked either of you about what you and my sister discussed, but I'm concerned about Melinda. She's not eating, cries at night, her sobs seeping under the door. I can't comfort her. When she first came here, she was inconsolable to a degree I've never seen in her since, well, you know."

"There wasn't much conversation. I tried to explain and apologize, but she was so upset that I couldn't get a word in. As you know, the worst thing you can do in these situations with her is interrupt and not let her say what she needs to get out first. But there was never an opportunity for me to respond; she just left."

Diane interrupted. "I don't know what you can do at this point. I'm very worried. As bad as she is now, I can't imagine what will happen when you leave.

"I can't change the fact that I will get orders for somewhere else, but it needn't be the end of our relationship if she gives me a chance. I want us to continue despite the challenges and the separation we will face. I love her, Diane."

Diane walked to the door but stopped when Scott called her name. "I'm grateful to you for letting me know how she is."

~ * ~

Scott was lying in bed, listening to a language tape given to him in class, repeating the pronunciations and intonations until a banging sound came from the wall facing Arthur's apartment. After a moment, he refocused on the tape. In a few minutes, a second bang startled him. "Arthur, what are you doing," he said, certain that his neighbor didn't hear. The next time, three smacks against the wall irritated him. Scott walked outside and knocked on Arthur's door. When there was no response, he put his ear against the wood and detected a weak sound resembling a groan. He pounded harder, shouting Arthur's name. Hal Tremont, who lived on the other side of Arthur's apartment, came out.

"What's the commotion?" he asked.

"I heard banging against the wall and knocked on Arthur's door without response. Something's wrong. Could you get Mrs. Redman? She must have a key to his apartment."

While Hal ran to the manager's apartment, Scott shouted, attracting other residents who came out to see what was happening. Hal said she was not in. Stepping back, Scott flew against the apartment door. The wood shook, but the lock held. In his second attempt, Scott heard the side near the hinges crack, followed by the door flying open. Once inside, he looked around and found Arthur on the floor near the wall in his bedroom. Rushing to Arthur's side, Scott placed his hand on the unconscious man's chest. By then, a crowd had gathered outside, peering into the broken opening when Scott yelled, "Call for an ambulance; he's still breathing." A tall, red-haired man pushed through the crowd to kneel beside Scott.

"I was a paramedic before joining up, Lieutenant." He pressed against Arthur's chest.

Scott cringed at the use of his rank but didn't sense sarcasm. Someone from the outside crowd called, "An ambulance is on the way."

Scott asked the former paramedic what he thought about Arthur's condition. The sailor answered, "In all likelihood, he had a heart attack. If you hadn't broken in, he probably would have died."

Within ten minutes, the paramedics charged toward the room, the crowd separating to let them in. Arthur, still unconscious, was carried out on a stretcher. Scott walked past the residents still murmuring over what had happened; a few cornered Hal for information. Before he could go inside his apartment, Scott felt a hand on his arm and saw it was Diane.

"How is he?"

"I don't know... still breathing, not conscious. I hope the hospital staff can reach his family."

Scott knew everyone thought highly of Arthur, but Diane probably knew him best, having brought him meals long before she added Scott to the list of recipients.

"You should go to the hospital and be there for him. I'll look for an address book inside to call his wife, since you made entering his apartment easier," she added.

"Why me?"

"He wanted you to go with him to get Jeff out of jail, so he obviously thinks highly of you. I know you don't think it, but he's not the only one, so go."

Scott closed his door and started for his car until he heard someone say to wait up. He saw Jeff running toward him, his long hair flying straight back.

"I want to go with you because Arthur was there for me."

When they got into Scott's car, Jeff said, "I know how to get to the hospital."

As they traveled, Jeff gave directions. "We're about five minutes away, Scott."

"It's good to hear someone, especially a guy, call me by my first name."

"Why not? I'm not military and have upset people at times. When Debbie and I arrived, many people in the apartment hesitated to befriend us—we were different, but they overcame their reluctance. They'll do so with you if you give them time."

"I don't have much time."

"That's the rub. You military people come and go so friendships don't last, even special ones," he glanced at Scott when he said that.

"So why did you move there, why stay?" Scott asked.

"The rent is cheap, which we figured when we learned most living there were in the service. We really liked being there and enjoyed the company of many nice couples. To be honest, we will also be moving out. I'm a carpenter, so I can work anywhere; you've probably seen some of Denise's beadwork, but she has other artistic skills that can be useful as a business anywhere. We won't remain here much longer. We're saving to buy a house someday or even build once we find land, which won't be in California because of the state's real estate cost. We'll raise non-conformist children and live off the soil as much as possible."

"Melinda has a beautiful bracelet Denise made that she loves. She tried to convince me to approach your wife about making one for men. Didn't think they would go well with a uniform."

"I won't ask you how things are between you two, but if there is still separation, I hope it will be resolved soon. You are two good people who should be together."

Scott was about to speak when Jeff interrupted. "Turn left here to the emergency room lot."

"You know your way the route pretty well."

"My talented wife uses sharp instruments to practice her craft. Need I say more?"

Once inside the emergency room, Scott asked the receptionist about Arthur's admission. The young woman was hesitant to provide information.

"We live in the same apartment complex with Arthur; his wife is setting up his home in another state after he retires. Someone will call his family to convey his condition. Right now, we are the only family he has here."

A tall, burly man walked toward them. He reminded Scott of a linebacker from his college football team. The receptionist mentioned the situation to him.

"I'm Doctor Renard. We're monitoring your friend. He had a heart attack. We'll be performing surgery in the morning, but he is resting comfortably now."

"Can we see him?" Jeff asked.

"I don't see why not. He's been transferred to room 133, which is down this hallway," he said, pointing. "Your friend is unconscious, though."

Scott and Jeff went to the room and stood before Arthur's bed. Monitors were attached to his chest; tubes were pinned to his arms.

Scott said, "Arthur, everyone in the apartments is worried about you. You're our token old man. We need you. The doctors here will fix your heart so you can come back. Diane will contact your wife to let her know. Meanwhile, rest; we'll check on you daily while you're here."

Scott looked at Jeff and saw his eyes were filling.

"Hey, buddy; this is Flower Child. Denise and I are so grateful for what you did to keep me from wearing prison stripes. We'll be there for you when you return."

On the way to the car, Scott asked. "Flower Child?"

Jeff said, "That's what he calls me, that and Hippie, to tease. Oh, wait. I have orders to call Debbie as soon as I see Arthur."

When they were back at the apartments, Scott saw Melinda standing outside his door. His heart jumped upon seeing her.

"It's so good to see you. How did you know I'd be back now?"

"Debbie stopped by to share her husband's call, including that you two were leaving the hospital. Diane did reach Arthur's wife to explain what had happened. She'll be flying out tomorrow; we'll pick her up to bring her here first, then to the hospital. I spoke to Mrs. Redman, who will have the door fixed quickly. Arthur's wife wanted us to share her gratitude for saving his life."

"Melinda, I wish you'd come inside so we can talk. I've been miserable without you. I want to explain, but more importantly, want your forgiveness."

"This not the time. Arthur is our only focus now. I'm still struggling, Scott, with such anger that I can't get past."

"You know I love you; the time away from you, knowing you're upset with me, has reminded me how much I care for and miss you."

Melinda started to cry. "I said I can't deal with this now." She ran to her apartment.

When Scott returned from class, he saw Diane and Mariam at Arthur's door talking to a tall, plump woman with dark hair sprinkled with gray. Diane introduced him to Rhonda, Arthur's wife.

"You were the one who found my husband and had him taken to the hospital," Rhonda said as she grabbed his hand to shake.

"We'll let you two talk," Diane said.

"Won't you come inside," Rhonda said, "I made coffee."

When Scott stepped inside, he saw a food tray on the table.

"I see the Welcome Wagon just left. I don't want to interrupt your dinner."

"I can heat the meal later; besides, I'm not that hungry right now."

They sat at the kitchen table and sipped the hot coffee.

"Even before you rescued my husband, he spoke highly of you. I'm so grateful to you and everyone here who has been good to Arthur, especially after we left to settle in our new home. Diane has been wonderful; I met her sister, Melinda, who was also kind, a sad young woman."

Scott flinched at the name. "How is Arthur?"

"He'll be recovering in the hospital for another few days. After a brief time at this apartment, Arthur will go with me to our new home. Diane and her sister have been taking me shopping and to the hospital so I can stay with him until he's ready to travel. The newspaper editor said Arthur could retire immediately with his full pension."

"We will miss him here, but I'm glad he'll be fine. He often talked about missing his family and how anxious he was to join you."

"I'm sure he will remember all of you fondly." Looking around the apartment, she added: "He didn't do much to the place. It looks austere."

"The same for my place. Like Arthur, I knew this was short term, but I will also miss the people here, even though most will probably be glad to see me go."

"Arthur told me about your..." she paused for the right word, "...dilemma. My husband also mentioned your problems about Melinda. He is such a gossip." She patted Scott's hand while she spoke. "I understand you'll be leaving in the near future, as are we. Plus, my husband's heart attack is a strong reminder of how short life can be and how unexpected changes can disrupt plans. On the flight here, I kept thinking that Arthur was planning to begin a new phase of his life in our new home, but he might not live to experience it." She took a deep breath. "I'm not the good judge of people my husband is, but I can sense Melinda is a special young woman—don't let her get away. Should I tell her what a wonderful man you are?"

Scott shook his head. "She's got to decide about me on her own, but thank you." He swallowed the last of the coffee and rose to leave. "I'll stop by the hospital tomorrow after class."

As he walked toward the door, Rhonda asked, "Who or what the heck is Flower Child?"

"That's Jeff, one of the residents. He and his wife, Debbie, are reminiscent of the hippies of the sixties. Arthur gave Jeff that name."

~ * ~

Scott visited Arthur at the hospital the following day and found him sitting up, talking to his wife. Rhonda rose and said, "I'm going to get some coffee."

"Don't go on my account," Scott said.

"I need the break. All morning, I've pleaded with my stubborn husband to stay here until the doctor gives him the approval to leave, but he's insistent on leaving tomorrow. Try to talk some sense into him."

"She lined up the people to her side; Jeff, a convert to her cause, was here this morning. Tell me what's going on at the apartments," Arthur said.

Scott said, "I'm the last person to be up on the activity there; that's usually your job."

"They're still mad at you?"

"Especially Melinda, which aches the most."

"I wish I could help. You need to sort out the discord between you and Melinda, but the rest of the folks there need to chill. They should have known you well enough to see you're a good guy. I'm living proof, literally."

"I saw Rhonda returning to the apartment yesterday with a couple of books and I noticed the title of one was about healthy eating. Your diet going to change."

"I'm sure—a lot of fruit, vegetables, with little or no dessert."

They talked for a while longer until his wife came back.

The next day, Rhonda knocked on Scott's door.

"I'm going to the hospital to take Arthur back to the apartment. Could you come with me if I have a problem getting him into the car? I mentioned his return to Diane so some of the couples could be here to welcome him. We'll take Arthur's car; I know my way around here, including to the hospital."

After signing the release papers, Rhonda wheeled Arthur out of his room to the lobby, where Scott was waiting. His help was unnecessary since Arthur could get around by himself, as was clear by his leap out of the wheelchair. When they arrived back at the apartments, a crowd had formed near the pool. As soon as Arthur, Rhonda, and Scott were in sight, they cheered. After displaying their affection for Arthur, the crowd looked toward Scott and continued clapping. Scott walked Arthur into his apartment. Once inside, he asked, "You did that for my benefit, didn't you?"

"You saved my life; that should overshadow any well-intended deception."

Scott returned to his apartment, recalling he'd not seen Melinda in the welcoming group.

Fifteen

On Wednesday, Arthur left after saying goodbye to Scott; a couple took over the apartment shortly after. When someone was at the door, he suspected one of his new neighbors had a question about the complex or the area. He was surprised to see Denise Fagella, Julie's maid of honor, standing before him. She was as attractive as he remembered, with tan skin and long auburn hair that constantly slipped forward to half cover her eye. For a moment, he stared until she spoke.

"Can I come in?" she asked.

Scott stepped aside while she reached down to grab a suitcase.

"I don't understand, Denise, why are you here?"

She explained. "I bought my plane tickets to visit Julie, but when I called her before leaving, Clay said she returned home unexpectedly due to her father's illness. I didn't know what to do—change my ticket to a later date, but I realized I had really come to see you. I am so sorry for not telling you I was engaged. We knew each other briefly, but I can't get you out of my mind."

"You said *was engaged*."

"I broke off the engagement, giving him back the ring. I spoke to Julie to ask if you'd forgiven me, but she discouraged me from trying to start anything with you. She wouldn't give me your address or telephone number as you requested. After a while, she gave me this address because I promised I would only write to you. I tried to honor that, but as you can see, I failed."

"Denise, you just can't come back into my life, expecting us to pick up as if nothing had happened. I can't be upset with you for deceiving me. In a much different way, I did the same to people in this apartment complex. However, I'm in a relationship—or hope I am—with someone I love."

"What do you mean, hope?"

"It's late. Have you had dinner?"

"No, I was too anxious to be hungry."

"Let's go to a local restaurant where I'll explain everything. I owe you that after you've made the trip, but nothing will change the fact that I am in love with someone else."

They went to a small restaurant in Pacific Grove, settling at a table until a waitress asked if they wanted anything to drink while handing them the menus. Scott ordered two glasses of Pinot Grigio.

"You look good, Scott. I've missed you. I wish Julie had told me you were involved with someone."

"I'm also surprised she didn't tell you; she was aware of the relationship."

"She did mention you were seeing someone but didn't indicate how serious it was."

After they ordered, Denise asked what he meant about deceiving people at the apartments.

"I didn't tell them I was an officer, which led them to think I was enlisted. I sustained the lie but eventually was discovered, alienating everyone, especially Melinda, the one I am or was in a relationship with."

"I don't understand the officer thing, but you're not seeing this woman now, then?"

"No, and I don't know if things will change before I get orders to leave."

"Maybe there is a chance for us."

"You live in a different state, and I'll be going somewhere likely out of the country. There were always limits to what there could be between us. You seemed to understand that before, using it as a reason we couldn't continue."

"I recall you said we'd work it out somehow. Also, doesn't the same problem exist with her after you move on?"

"Yes, it does. She lives in another state, too. We knew the time would come when she would go home, and I would report to my next duty station, but we were focused on the present."

"Then how is that different with me?"

"The difference is that I love her. I don't know what you and I could have been if we'd tried to see each other, traveled back and forth, or spoke on the phone, but that didn't happen. I can't compare what could have happened with you to what has happened with Melinda."

Denise said, "We both have lost something because of a lie, so I won't lie to you now. If we could see what could happen between us, that you could love me eventually, I'd call my boss about staying here with you for a week, or even two, returning after that. We would figure out the rest, but at least we'd be trying. I'm not going to die of a broken heart if rejected, but I do know you could be an important part of my life, someone I could love."

They finished their meals, both leaving half the food on the plate.

"Scott, can you take me to a hotel, not the one I stayed at when we—. There are too many memories there. I'll change my flight ticket for tomorrow."

"It's late, your suitcase is in my apartment, and I have a spare bedroom. You can change your flight there. Since tomorrow is Saturday, I don't have a class and can take you to the airport. It's best we don't mention this to Julie; knowing her, she'll blame herself for not doing something to prevent this awkwardness, even though she has nothing to feel guilty about."

Denise said, "You're right. Julie thinks she can solve everyone's problems. I know she cares for both of us. You should have heard the tongue-lashing I got when I called after the wedding. She was right to be upset with me and was angry with herself for not warning you before we got too involved. Clay is a lucky guy, as is Melinda if she comes to her senses."

"If you're ready to go, we'll head back to my place. I'm glad to see you."

When they got up from the table, Denise hugged him.

Arriving at the apartments, Scott parked in the back lot to avoid being seen. As he closed the door, he felt they had been undetected.

"Neither of us ate much tonight; can I get you something?" Scott asked.

"No, I'm fine, but a drink would be appreciated."

He took a bottle of Merlot from the cabinet and poured it into two glasses, handing her one. Scott sat on the couch while Denise settled on the soft chair.

"Why now?" he asked. "A lot of time has gone by since the wedding."

Denise sipped from the glass before answering. "I had to sort through a lot. Sometimes, the person most difficult to understand is ourselves. Was that night with you a fling or a sign of something more serious? Was I attracted to you enough to risk my relationship with Richard? I know I can be flirtatious, but I never would have gone that far with you on a whim or for a one-time roll in the sack. In the end, I knew that I didn't love Richard enough to marry him. But along the way, I considered going through with the wedding so I wouldn't hurt him or disappoint the families and friends. While the ceremony was months away, many of my family were enjoying the preparation. Eventually, I realized that logic was wrong; I couldn't ask him to wed someone who wasn't totally in love with him. Then I thought about you. As I pondered all the issues about marrying, I kept returning to you and the brief time we had together, not just in bed. I was attracted to you, though while I couldn't call it love, I knew my feelings for you would grow as we spent more time together."

"How did he react when you told him, and did you include what happened between us?"

"At first, I tried to avoid that; however, I realized I'd been dishonest enough. Also, Richard was willing to give us more time. At that point, I had to bring us up. He was further hurt but accepted that we couldn't be with each other. Did Melinda know what happened between you and me?"

"Yes, I told her. She asked how I felt about you but wasn't upset since we weren't seeing each other then."

Denise's eyebrows raised. "What did you tell her about us?"

"I said we met at Julie and Clay's wedding, that you were beautiful, and we got involved for a brief. period."

"By involved, did you explain we had sex, rather great sex?"

"No, but that was likely implied. I also mentioned you were engaged but never told me."

"We both hurt someone by our falsehoods."

"Falsehood! I came up with so many synonyms for a lie; that's one I never considered. My lie was one of commission, yours one of omission."

"Does that make a difference?"

"I don't know what to use to measure the difference; all I know is we both were wrong."

Denise rose from her chair and sat next to Scott on the couch. Scott fidgeted and removed her hand when she touched his thigh.

"I'm sorry; guess I had too much wine. Do you mind if I take a shower?"

He answered with a nod, and she walked into the bedroom. Within a few minutes, she came out and approached Scott, "Where are the towels?" The bathrobe was slightly open, and he could see her legs and part of her buttocks when she turned. Scott heard the sound of the water striking her naked skin and slapped his forehead to rid the thoughts forming in his mind. The water was off, and within a few minutes, she came out of the bathroom, barely covered by the towel, which dropped to the floor in front of the door to the bedroom.

Wide awake, Scott entered his bedroom and started reading a book, not absorbing the words. Later, he took off his clothes, all but his shorts, and slipped under the thin blanket. The moonless sky offered little illumination through the window over his bed. He dozed off but was startled by a touch on his arm; Scott shot up, his eyes half closed. Denise was sitting on the edge of his bed. She leaned over and kissed him. She was wearing a sheer nightgown, her breasts visible through the transparent cloth.

"We can't do this. You're asking me to repeat what happened the last time, but too much has changed."

"Do you want to give up the certainty of what we could have for the possibility of what you might have with Melinda?"

"Yes, I do."

She touched his cheek. "I had to try. Goodnight, Scott. See you in the morning."

He had difficulty falling asleep, tossing and turning until dawn. The smell of brewing coffee seeped under the door. He grabbed a bathrobe from the closet and walked to the kitchen. He saw Denise, fully dressed, her suitcase in the living room.

"I'm sorry about my failed seduction."

As he sat at the kitchen table across from her, Scott said, "Sorry about the seduction or that it failed?"

"Both, more the latter. I traveled a distance to win you back, so I had to keep trying. I wish we could stay friends, but that might not be the best. I want to ask a favor; again, don't tell Julie I was here. I've lost you, and I don't want to lose her as well."

Scott agreed. "I'll take you to the airport... just give me time to get dressed."

"Before you do, were you tempted last night?"

Scott didn't answer.

When they were ready to leave, Scott opened the door slightly, scanning the area for anyone outside. Grabbing her suitcase, he stepped outside. Denise put her arm through his. As they walked out, he saw Melinda out of the corner of his eye; he swiveled but glanced at her, as she rushed behind a door that quickly closed.

On the trip to the airport, he was distracted, wondering what Melinda might have seen or thought. Would her imagination lead her to believe he'd started another relationship? Now more than ever, he needed to meet with her, talk to her, and explain.

"Is there something on your mind, Scott? You've been very quiet since we left the apartment."

"No, I'm fine."

After parking, he walked her inside and waited at the gate of her flight.

"I'm not sorry I came; now I can move on with my life, including going to law school. I won't forget you."

She kissed him before walking toward the boarding ramp.

Sixteen

Scott called or hoped to encounter Melinda for a week but was unsuccessful. In his last effort to reach her by phone, he dialed the number, and Luke picked up.

"I was trying to reach Melinda to explain."

"She's not here, Scott. I'll tell her you called, but I doubt that will change anything."

"It's good to talk to *you*. We haven't for a while."

"Obviously, I was pissed when we learned you are an officer, but I realized it was not intended to harm. Besides, my wife supports you and influenced me to let the anger go. She changed the minds of others as well, especially after what you did for Arthur. Besides, people have been discussing what Diane calls *your hound dog face,* showing your regrets. She won't interfere with what's happening between you and Melinda, leaving her sister to work things out."

"I just wish I could talk to her."

"Like Diane, I don't want to get in the middle, but you should know Melinda plans to leave soon. I don't know the date or the reason for the sudden decision, except I learned she was upset over some woman leaving your apartment one morning."

Scott groaned. "That's a misunderstanding I need to explain. Thank you, Luke, for telling me and talking to me. I've missed your friendship."

Melinda never called or stopped by. When the phone rang, Julie was on the line. They spoke for a while.

"Clay is playing golf, so I'm coming over there alone."

When she arrived, she hugged him before closing the door. They talked for over an hour, and she embraced him in the doorway on the way out of his apartment.

~ * ~

The next day, Scott was peering into his refrigerator, mulling over his conversation with Julie, considering what else to do to reach Melinda, when the door flew open. The bottle of juice he held in his hand dropped to the floor, spilling the contents knocked down by Melinda leaping into his arms. They kissed deeply, pausing only to catch their breaths with no need for words, her tears salting her lips. Scott stepped back, wiping the tears from her cheeks with his thumbs, staring at her face.

"I've missed you so much," he said. "I'm reluctant to ask... what caused you to change your mind."

She giggled, "Why reluctant?"

"I don't really care to know why if it will disrupt the moment."

Melinda grabbed his hand, took him to the couch, and explained her meeting with Julie.

"I'd seen you with another woman a few days ago. Diane and I were walking toward our apartment when we saw a second woman leave your apartment. I said, 'Another one! He is sure getting over me. Is he auditioning?'

"That was Julie; the first was Denise," Scott exclaimed.

"She heard me, realizing what I'd said, and called my name. She walked toward me and Diane. 'How did you know who I am?' I asked, 'Did Scott tell you about our relationship as part of his technique?'"

"Technique? I don't have a technique," he said.

Melinda kissed him. "Are you going to let me finish the story?"

"Sorry; go ahead."

"She introduced herself as Julie, your friend. I said, 'My god! Scott has mentioned you often. He was part of your wedding party.' She wanted to talk to me, but not in an open area. Diane had said she was going to visit Bridget in apartment 162. I knew Luke was waiting for his car to get fixed at the garage, so I invited her back to the apartment. I put on the coffee pot, and we sat at the table. I don't recall her words exactly, but she told me you've been miserable since we separated and that you deeply regret the deception. Apparently, she warned you, but you kept stalling. I told her I knew that but asked her why you wouldn't trust me, even if keeping it from everyone else, thinking she might have more insight."

"I was amused by her response: 'Because he's male. They don't think like we women do.' She added that you are perceptive in some ways and clueless in others. 'He's a good person who loves you very much.' I remembered those words exactly. I apologized for misjudging her but explained that I had seen him leading another woman out of his apartment early one morning and strongly suspected she was there for the night. Her eyes rolled back, and she said she needed to explain, asking for another cup of coffee first. After a few sips, she continued.

"I'm paraphrasing, but I think I'm pretty close. She said she believed I knew about your involvement with her best friend and maid of honor, who was engaged when she came here for the ceremony but never told you. Julie thought you two had a harmless flirtation. It was more than that she learned and was angry with her maid of honor and herself for not telling you before things happened. You wouldn't talk to the bridesmaid once you learned she was getting married; she thought it was over. Julie got a call from the woman, Denise, saying she wanted to visit, mentioning nothing about a desire to see you. They set a day for her to fly down, but Julie had to return home unexpectedly. Instead of changing the flight, Denise came anyway, primarily to see you. She stayed overnight in the other bedroom and went home the next morning, which is likely when I saw her leaving. Julie said her friend was honest; she tried to seduce you but failed. Denise wanted to keep Julie from knowing, but guilt took over, and she came clean when she got home. What Julie said next, I can quote: 'You may still be mad at Scott for his lie, but don't hold Denise's deviousness against him.' I told her I was glad she told me all this, and if we hadn't had that conversation, I'd never have known. Her next words stunned me; she started by saying, 'There's one more thing I need to share with you.'

"At first, I couldn't say anything; my eyes filled, and Julie came to my side of the table and hugged me. I bawled. I explained that we both knew the day would come, but it was still a shock. Suddenly, I realized you could leave without knowing how much I love you, and I would go home convinced you would soon forget about me."

"What did she say that made you change your mind, although I'm certain I know?"

Melinda paused; Scott could see she was on the edge of upset. "She told me you got orders to report in three weeks. Where are you going?"

"I report to the base in Coronado here in California. While land based, I'll be assigned to ships in the Pacific."

"We need to make plans, then."

Scott asked, "What do you mean by plans?"

"I haven't had much time to think about everything, but I need to call my boss, rescinding my notice that I would be back to work next week, committing to returning after three weeks. Next, I need to talk to Diane, filling her in on my conversation with Julie, including my leaving their apartment to move in with you. I want to be with you every minute I can for that three-week period. I'm assuming you don't mind," she added coyly.

"I'll help you move your stuff. When do you want to start?"

"Right now," she said, grabbing his hand, feigning movement toward the door, instead pulling him to the bedroom. She swept aside the clothes he'd left on top of the bed, rolled down the bedspread, and jumped on the mattress, waiting for him to join her. They stripped quickly. Kissing, they faced each other with their arms in a tight embrace. They were sitting up, she in his lap, her legs wrapped around him. Scott lifted Melinda, turning her so she was lying face up, his hands at the base of her head while he settled her down.

"I've missed you; I've missed your body and missed making love with you," Scott said afterward.

She was leaning toward him, her elbow pressing into the mattress, her hand resting on his open hand. "Never talk about what kept us apart, not discuss the future, only what we'll do for three weeks, which will include much of this." She was grinning. "I love you," Melinda whispered in his ear.

"I love you, too. How do you think Diane will react to your announcement?"

"Surprised. I'd planned to get far away from you the last time she and I spoke. Now look at us. Diane has always liked you, so I don't believe she'll be upset. Once I explain everything, she'll be convinced. Scott, would you have rejected the bridesmaid if you were certain we weren't getting back together or if we'd never met?"

"Her name is—"

"I know her name, and don't deflect."

"You just listed the *nevers,* want to add another: never discuss—*what ifs.*"

"Deal, with one condition: I get to see you in your uniform."

"Now? Wouldn't you rather see me in my current condition?"

"I've had enough of that. I haven't seen you in your officer garb, so go to it, Lieutenant."

Scott got up from the bed, picked up his underwear from the floor, took his uniform from the closet, and dressed. After he finished, he stood in front of her.

"The hat, too."

"We call it my cover; get used to Navy terminology."

"I'm impressed. I've made love to a Navy lieutenant."

"Lieutenant j.g.," he corrected. "That's a rank lower than lieutenant."

"Not to me. Diane will be looking for me; this will likely be the last place she expects I'll be."

As she was dressing, the phone rang.

"Yes, Diane, she's here. Melinda will explain everything as soon as she—" He caught himself, changing the sentence, "can."

He looked at Melinda, who was covering her mouth until he hung up. She kissed him, dressed, and left. Scott shook his head, saying to himself, "What just happened?"

After a few hours, Melinda returned carrying a change of clothes and a makeup case.

"This will be for tomorrow only, after which I get the rest of my stuff while you're in class. Later, we need to make a schedule for the remaining time."

He grabbed her, lifting Melinda slightly off the ground "Plans, schedules, on a day that we're just back together. I want to savor the time, not strategize."

"I'm serious; I don't want to waste a minute on something unimportant or keep us apart even briefly."

"Okay, are you going to post the POD?"

"What's that?"

"I said you need to learn the Navy lingo; it means plan of the day, which contains every evolution of that day."

"Very funny; we needn't go to that extreme. Let me start. We'll wake up together, have breakfast—which I'll make sometimes, and you do as well—I'll stay out of the bathroom while you get ready for class. I'll make the bed, clean up, and make a list of food items we need that you can pick up at the commissary. On the weekend, we can clean; why am I doing this since we have so few weekends." Tears formed on the edge of her eyes.

When they were in bed together that night, Melinda leaned against him. Scott could hear the pace of his heartbeat quicken when he rubbed her naked back.

"Scott, I don't want to give up a day with you, but don't you want to spend time with your family before you report?"

"I haven't told them yet."

"You should see them; they'll be hurt if you don't, especially if they know you are spending the final time with me. I can arrange the flight while you're in class."

"I have a few days more than three weeks; I can take four days with them, including the travel time. I hate giving up any days with you, but it is the right thing. My classes are winding down, with final exams in two weeks. I'll take a few leave days and visit them. Why don't you come with me?"

"I'd love to meet your folks, but this is when you should see them alone. I would be a distraction. There will be another time."

His flight was scheduled for Friday, returning on Monday. He arranged a car service to take him to the airport on the departure date.

While waiting out front with Melinda, he said, "Please don't wreck my car," as he handed her the keys.

They kissed as the taxi pulled up. While he was away, they spoke on the phone frequently; he described the reunion involving immediate family and other relatives, mentioning their relationship frequently to everyone. Melinda said she stayed at her sister's while he was gone. Missing him so much, staying at his apartment while he was gone was too upsetting.

Melinda picked him up at the airport and drove him back to the apartments in his car after they had dinner. Since Scott had a class the following day, they went to bed early, and after making love, Scott offered more details about the visit to his family.

"Lilly had told everyone she'd met you and said you were good for me. Later, she pulled me aside and wanted to know what happened when I revealed my rank. Lilly is also leaving soon for her job on the West Coast, so in some ways, that was a farewell occasion for both of us and possibly the only time we will all meet for a while. Needless to say, my parents are sorry to see us both go. What happened here?"

"Two couples left, the Wrightmans and the Lindermans. Apparently, your class is not the only one finishing the course, and five more families are leaving before the end of the month. Their apartments have already been rented, probably by students just beginning their programs. Some residents, especially Jeff and Debbie, asked where you were. I also learned we are back as the leading topic of gossip and speculation since I moved in with you."

"I heard there is a dinner at the officer's club, including dancing. It would be nice to embrace you in a vertical position. It will be another introduction into the life of an officer."

"You mean exposure to how the other half lives. I feel like the poor scrub woman who has been invited to the royal ball, a Cinderella adventure."

"It's not like that. I want you in my life, Melinda, not just for a few more weeks. I can't envision my life without you, and this is part of the world that goes with the territory if it is what you want and is best for you."

"What are you saying?"

"We hinted at staying connected after I left for my assignment, and I've said that I want you in my life no matter what logistical difficulties we meet. I spoke to my detailer—he's the person who arranges my assignment—and without getting into the specifics, he said I would be at sea for a 'considerable period.' How unfair might it be to ask you to wait for me to return from wherever I go? I don't know where I'll be, when I'll get back, or how I may be out of touch for a while. We've been together in a confined space—this apartment complex—with a fixed routine. We love each other, but the obstacles are the ones we, that is I, create. I didn't sleep much last night. Having you alongside me was great, but I suddenly realized how selfish that feeling was. I missed you so much when we were separated; I knew you felt the same way. How can I put you through more upset because I have an obligation to the Navy that will keep us apart for a lot longer? You said Teddy and I were not alike, but we are similar in that we brought or will bring, in my case, pain in your life unintentionally. Are you better off putting both of us in your past?"

"Scott, the obstacles were not only from you. I should have let you explain and talked to you instead of ranting. Don't link yourself with Teddy; you have helped me get over the loss. I was angry about your rank, but now I'm proud. But I'm not leaving you, no matter what happens. Unless they send you out to sea for a decade, I'll wait. We can never discuss this issue again. We are together now, and we will stay that way in the future. I'd gladly attend an event at the officer's club with you, even if it is the last occasion for a long time."

~ * ~

They dressed separately, and she used the spare room. When they finished, Scott opened the door wearing a tan suit, yellow dress shirt, and mixed-color tie. Waiting in the small living room for her to come out, he sat on the couch. When she entered, Melinda was in a short red dress, high-heeled shoes, and a white sweater thrown over her shoulder. For a moment, he stared at her with an admiring look.

He kissed her. "You are gorgeous," he said, his mouth against her neck.

Melinda giggled. "Are you sure you want to go out? I took time to dress, but I can undress quickly."

Stepping back, he frowned. "We should go." Taking her hand, he led her out of the apartment to the side parking lot. She said she was nervous on the drive to the Post Graduate Officers' Club. Patting her thigh, he assured her she would outshine any woman there, and the men would be envious.

"They're not all active-duty Navy. Some government civilians take courses there, but no one will wear their rank on their sleeves or ribbons on their chests. They will look like any group of people at a modestly fancy dinner."

Entering the cavernous building, they saw rows of tables lined with food, some with cooking staff standing in front of generous portions of meat waving large knives and forks. Plates of potatoes steamed in burner-heated trays. Stacked plates, along with rolled-up napkins holding utensils, were on the first table. A bar was at the room's far end, with lines of men and women waiting to order drinks from white-coated bartenders.

"Should we get in the line for food?" Melinda asked.

"First, we should get a table; I hope you don't mind sitting with strangers. It's pretty crowded here."

Scott's eyes fixed on a table to his right. Taking her hand, he walked to see familiar faces standing and smiling as they approached. Melinda screeched so loudly she quickly covered her mouth. "Julie!" She threw her arms around her while nodding to Clay.

"I wouldn't be here with him if it weren't for you."

After introducing Clay to Melinda, Julie said. "Sit and join me while our men get us drinks."

The two women sat next to each other.

"Scott didn't tell me you would be here. I assume he knew."

"He not only knew, he arranged it, including giving us a head start so we would get a table. We spoke briefly when he called, and I've never heard him so happy now that you two are back together."

"I don't know if he told you, but I was getting ready to go home, even bought the flight tickets. This would have turned out differently if I hadn't seen you that day."

The men came back with Scott carrying two glasses of white wine while Clay held one glass. Sitting down, Clay offered to make a toast. "To couples at the edge of a new adventure."

The three sipped wine, and Julie drank from a water glass. Melinda looked at her new friend.

"You're drinking water; are you pregnant?"

Julie looked at Clay. "I haven't been to a doctor yet, but I'm pretty sure."

Melinda reached over to hug her; Scott and Clay shook her hands.

"Did you know, Scott?" Melinda asked.

"No, I'm learning this the same time you are."

"But you will leave here, maybe even before the baby is born."

"Honey, this is Navy life. Clay may make this a career, and if we wait for the best timing, I'd have a baby at forty."

They rose to get dinner and stood in the line winding to the back wall. Clay patted his wife's stomach. "Take larger portions; you're eating for two."

Melinda whispered to Scott, "Is there a message for us in their happiness?"

"Yes, that uncertainty is very often a factor in life's choices, whether or not I stay in the Navy. They will make it work, and we will, too, if that's what we both want."

Melinda grinned. "Maybe I should get pregnant to show that I want us to be together always?"

"I have enough challenges dealing with you; two would drive me insane," he joked.

Melinda looked toward Julie when they returned; "How did you two meet?"

"Clay and I were from the same town, so we dated before he was assigned to language school. I have relatives nearby, allowing me to move down here. Although, as Scott and another roommate you've not met, Mark, could attest, I was often at their place. We both loved the area and decided we would marry in Monterey. Clay can explain the early living arrangements and the timing. I got a job locally to help build our finances for the future."

Clay took the cue. "I was assigned to a class erroneously, one that had already started. The next offering was about six weeks later. I worked at the school in various administrative roles, none especially taxing. I learned about the vacancy in the house Mark and Scott rented. As a result of the initial delay, we have a while before leaving Monterey."

A five-piece band played while couples interrupted their dining to dance. Scott and Melinda pushed through the crowd to a spot near the music and held each other. Their steps began with broad movements, then slowed to nearly standing still. Her arms were around his neck, pulling his head closer so that he rested his chin on her head.

"I'm delighted we got to hear Julie's great news. Promise me we will never lose touch with them, no matter where our lives take us. I also realized that Naval officers aren't so scary."

"We won't disconnect from Julie and Clay ever," Scott said.

The couples stayed for hours, selecting dessert; Julie justified two pieces of chocolate cake with the excuse of eating for two.

Leaving together, they all hugged and got into their cars, but not before Julie invited Melinda and Scott to their house in the future. On the drive, Melinda leaned on Scott's shoulder.

"I really enjoyed tonight, and I'm looking forward to going back to the apartment and making love."

Clothes were scattered from the front door to the edge of the bedroom. When they separated, Melinda sat on the edge of the bed and cried.

Scott rubbed her bare back. "Why so sad on such a wonderful evening."

"Because tonight was so special; because I love you so much, I never want to be away from you. I looked around the room and thought that many couples there could go through what we have in front of us—being apart. I'm scared. I'm not as strong as Julie or Diane."

"I know how you feel. You were outside my life, then part of my life, now you are my life. What's difficult for me is that we have been inseparable these last days, and in a short time, we'll be separated for a much longer period."

~ * ~

Scott left his apartment the following day and sat on a folding chair by the pool. Melinda had dinner with her sister to discuss returning home. The evening fog flowed out of the woods across from the apartments, swallowing the clear air over the complex. Melinda came out of Diane's apartment and Scott stood to get a nearby chair.

"I don't need it," she said.

Melinda sat on his lap, putting her arms around his neck.

"Why don't we go to my apartment?" he asked.

Pressing her head against his neck, she said, "If we did, I'd want to make love with you, but I can't physically or emotionally. Do you understand?"

"Yes," he answered.

Melinda settled back against him while he looked at the shrouded moon, ignoring the moisture in the surrounding fog. After a long time of saying little, he could feel her embrace weakening; she was slowly falling asleep. Scott kissed her forehead to wake her.

They walked back to his apartment and fell quickly asleep, but not before Scott said, "I'll see you tomorrow, my sleeping beauty."

They played tourists over the next few days, visiting the Carmel Mission, Cannery Row, and Seventeen Mile Drive. Carmel by the Sea was their favorite location, and they went there often. They also went horseback riding, Melinda on her favorite horse, Alexander. By the last week, Scott had completed his course and could spend time solely with Melinda. Diane invited them over two days before Scott was to leave. She and Luke were gracious and treated him as if nothing of the past had happened. On the last night, Scott offered to take Melinda out to dinner, but she was hesitant, making vague excuses. When his phone rang, she hurried to pick up the receiver. After she hung up, Scott asked who that was, and she answered that Diane called, without more explanation.

"I changed my mind," she said, "let's go out to eat."

Stepping outside, Scott saw a crowd gathered in the pool area, everyone looking at him. Looking at Melinda, he asked, "What's happening?"

"They want to say goodbye."

Stepping down from his apartment, Scott was greeted by handshakes and hugs. They all used his first name, which he realized was the best indicator that all was forgiven. Debbie pushed through the group and nearly leaped toward Scott, catching him in a strong embrace. Jeff was close behind her, smiling. Afterward, the residents moved to the food assembled on several folding tables, pausing to let Scott and Melinda have the first choice. Many asked Scott about his duty station, while some women asked Melinda what she planned to do.

"I'm going home to regain my job and wait until I can next see him," she nodded toward Scott.

After the residents drifted back to their apartments, Scott and Melinda went back to his. Sitting on the couch, they discussed the final steps.

"On Thursday, someone from the Navy will pick up my car to have it shipped. I'll take a cab to the airport for the flight to San

Diego. I dropped off the car keys with Mrs. Redman, so they needn't bother you. I'll be on the base there for a few days before being assigned to a cruiser. I have your home address and will write you instructions on how to write back. I told Mrs. Redman I'd leave the few things I added—pots, pans, plates, and utensils; none are of much value. As you've said, there is nothing especially personal here. Give Mrs. Redman the front door key when you're ready. The only valuable part of the apartment I wish I could take with me is you."

Melinda was crying as he spoke. Scott embraced her and, to distract her, asked about her plans.

"I have my plane ticket for next week. I'll move my stuff to keep in Diane's until my flight. I can't stay in this apartment for even one night after you leave. I can't believe the time has come, the day I dreaded since we've been together. When I first started going out with you, I expected ours to be a short-term relationship, never expecting what you would become to me, never predicting that I would love you so much."

Both slept little, each looking at the clock on the nightstand or the window for signs that the sun was beginning its ascent. Scott suggested she stay with her sister instead of with him the last night to spare both the pain of saying goodbye. But she had refused. While he showered and dressed, she made breakfast of eggs and toast. As they sipped coffee, the phone rang; Scott told her the car service was out front. Melinda walked with him to the lot, holding his hand. Scott gave his suitcase and duffel bag to the driver, who placed them in the trunk. Melinda was crying as the car pulled away, waving until she could no longer see them. Scott took a handkerchief from his pocket and dabbed at his eyes.

Seventeen

Scott arrived at the base in San Diego, a massive complex of over 1,600 acres with piers extending into the ocean's edge with vessels of all classes, including aircraft carriers, combat ships, and support boats. He reported to the central command, where he was assigned to temporary quarters in the bachelor officer housing with a directive to report to the cruiser USS Syracuse in a week. For the days prior, he attended briefings on the planned deployment.

During his orientation, he met the sixteen assigned enlisted men who'd reported aboard a few days before him. One of the sailors, Seaman O'Connell, had been in language class while Scott was there, but had completed his studies a few months before. On the day the ship left the pier, Scott stood on the bridge watching the captain and officer of the deck maneuver the vessel through the crowded docks and shallow water into the deep, vast ocean. Staring at the sea, Scott thought of Melinda, wondering what she was doing, missing her, and remembering when she was beside him in bed. During the preparation period before boarding, he'd called her several times, giving her an address to reach him and warning her that mail deliveries would be infrequent once they departed port. In his room, which he shared with a supply officer, he taped a picture she'd given him to the metal frame of his bunk.

After weeks at sea, a helicopter landed on the back of the ship with mail for the crew. A navy chief brought the letters to the officers' lounge to distribute. Scott received correspondence from his sister, Julie, and Melinda. Putting two envelopes on the table, he ripped open Melinda's letter first.

Scott,

We talked at length about how difficult being apart like this would be, but the emptiness and loneliness I feel is far beyond what I could have imagined. I can't get you off my mind; I'm restless at night, missing being with you, touching you, and feeling the warmth of your skin, knowing that you love me. I envision you sailing further and further away to a destination you probably can't share, worried that you could be in danger at some point. Not knowing where you are or how you are is unbearable. I'm certain you will be back, which offers some comfort. We will be together, and our lives will be only interrupted but not disrupted.

I am trying to keep busy. After returning to work, I was given added responsibilities, which offered distraction because, in the inactive times, my thoughts automatically drifted back to you.

Now for the news updates on the Pacific Grove apartments. Diane and Luke are fine and awaiting his orders he expects to arrive in the near future. Diane talks about how anxious she and Luke are to move on and go to their next duty station. Last week, I got a phone call from Julie. We had a long talk; as you might guess, you were often the topic of discussion. I love her. She made me laugh and cry in the same conversation. Jeff and Debbie left the apartments after buying property in some remote area where they plan to grow their own food (and probably pot). Arthur contacted my sister, and he's back to total health, receiving close attention from his nurse/wife. I would give anything to stay in California with you even if we never left the apartment. But, of course, that's not practical. You didn't join the Navy to be stuck in an apartment.

Are you going to visit foreign ports eventually? I hope you don't fall in love with local women. You are not very good at restraint, as I recall when we were in bed (ha, ha, I hope no censors are reading your mail).

I'm back in my room at my parents' house, at my old job, meeting family and friends as before: people who know me, my life, even my time with Teddy, but they don't know you. I show them the photograph of us that Diane took, but they see you as this flat image, not the flesh and blood man I know, the man who loves me and I love. Talking about you gives them a better awareness of you, but I can never give them an accurate sense of you through words—they need to see you, hear you, and grasp why I love you so much.

Once, I woke from a deep sleep and wondered if I had dreamed it all. Were Pacific Grove, the apartments, the couples who lived there, you, all real? I quickly realized it was all true; everything happened as I remembered, and the memories with you are real.

Please write. I need to know how you are doing, how you are feeling, if you're safe, and if you are missing me. I hope this letter reaches you soon, reminding you that I'm waiting for you and that moment I can hold you again.

I love you,
Melinda

Scott was uplifted by her letter, knowing she felt the separation as he did, and her outlook was hopeful. In addition, he was glad she had eased back into a comfortable and familiar routine surrounded by family, friends, and co-workers. Like her, he missed the life they had together in the apartments. She was correct that they couldn't stay that way; nonetheless, that period was not the actual military, where separation is common and, at times, unpredictable. Decisions about his future were simpler when the choices only affected him; now, he had to consider her in future career plans. He had heard stories of women who leaped into marriage with sailors only to realize that life was not what they wanted. He remembered Melinda's telling of a young wife in the apartments who doubted her union with a sailor. Would doubts form for Melinda as time passed; would she become so immersed in her surroundings at home that she would be reluctant to be part of the uncertainty of Navy life?

He wrote to her and shared his feelings about the separation, repeating his love for her. However, letters were insufficient; he needed to talk to her and touch her. When they were together, especially in his apartment, they rarely talked without touching or holding each other's hands. Her expressions while speaking added dimension to the words, and her eyes revealed her emotions vividly.

Melinda,
I miss you so much. Life at sea varies from intense to periods of solitude, but regardless of what I'm doing or what's happening around me, I think of you. Last night, I

went on the ship's bridge on a moonless night, intensifying the darkness. Even in the emptiness of the sea around us, I thought of you during the nights we were in my apartment with the lights off and the blinds drawn so we relied solely on touch so I could feel the skin of your breasts and hips (sorry, censors, if you exist). We are both tactile. But there was no escaping memories of you in daylight when I recalled your beautiful face, your smile, and the look in your eyes when you were planning to do something devious. Your attractiveness was not diminished even by sadness or upset. Although I admit your angry face is troubling (ha, ha). Those eyes are so haunting, so revealing; you'd make a poor card shark or arrested criminal. We've talked often about our lives before we met, but I feel there is much more to learn about you and what your friends were like (then and now).

When I'm having a meal or on the bridge with other officers, they often talk about times with their spouses. I'm sure some memories have faded for them. Mine are so recent and few in comparison, although perhaps more vivid. I recall the first time I held your hand—the touch felt like I'd put my fingers in a live socket. When you embraced me, I sensed the warmth extending from your arms to my entire back. Our first kiss (which caught me off guard!) was jolting and sensual. I remember the first time in bed with you; you said it was not the first we'd done so, but the first time with each other. But for me, it was the first time I could consider intimate, a sense of fusion as if our bodies were made to blend.

I can't share where I am or what we are doing, but know I am safe. Periodically, we do go to foreign ports, and no, I haven't met exotic women. When I'm in those locations, I only think about how much more enjoyable they would be if shared with you.

The officers on board are great, and I have a capable team. It's odd to have gone from a land-based school to an ocean-going vessel. Monterey and Pacific Grove seem distant.

I'm glad you've been in touch with Julie. I also hope she and Clay will stay in our lives despite distance challenges. I enjoyed the latest on some of the couples we knew at the apartments. Despite her initial caution about our relationship, Diane has greatly supported us. I hope to meet your parents and spend time with your friends one day. I'm sure they have some stories to tell about you.

I have to end this letter. I want to get it out with the next chopper.

I love you, Melinda.

Scott

He dropped off his letter to the ship's post office, a small square space, and noticed the bundle of bagged mail in the corner prepared for the next pickup. His letter would likely go into the half-filled bag and be added to the stack. He was on the forecastle when the helicopter arrived. The mailbags were loaded for transfer to a supply ship and eventually to a base. Scott envisioned the route his correspondence would take to reach her and be held in her anxious hands.

~ * ~

Over the next few months, they exchanged letters, repeating their love for each other and expressing their impatient need to be together again. The ardor of her emotions, as apparent in her wording, never changed. However, Scott thought he detected changes in how she talked about her activities and involvements. She'd found an apartment she could afford and detailed the additions to her new place: furniture, wall postings, and kitchen utensils. Friends helped her to paint rooms, followed by a post-painting celebration of pizza. As he feared, their lives, which were so intertwined in the apartments, were becoming so divergent that giving up what they had now gotten through their separate careers and locations might be difficult, especially for her.

Scott was surprised when a letter came from Diane. After the typical greeting and update on her life with Luke, she got to the purpose of her letter.

I fibbed to Melinda when I last spoke to her, saying that I wanted to send you a card for your coming birthday; that's not the reason for this letter, although I wish you a happy birthday. Of course, as you can imagine, you are a frequent topic of conversation when we speak on the phone. She settled into her job, enjoying her role along with interacting with so many people she knew. Since coming home, she's made new friends, spending weekends in 'girl activities.' Surprisingly, my sister joined a volleyball team through a local sponsoring organization. She is happy, except that she misses you. Melinda sees her life as content in a limited regional area while your life has crossed borders extending to foreign, exotic countries, which will be part of your life for the duration of your time in the Navy. Lately, she has been wistful about your future together, primarily because she feels she would be depriving you of experiences that you can enjoy better unencumbered. My dear sibling is more selfless than I could be in many ways. Melinda is in a better place than she has been for a long while, getting past, while not forgetting, Teddy's death. If she is right that you would be best to delay any commitment to her or any woman until you've had a chance to enjoy what the Navy can offer, then now is the time to break it off. I want to be clear: she loves you very much and will be heartbroken. Equally, if you still love her, she will be thrilled.

But I don't know what you think. Maybe you feel she would be better off in her current life and situation. Familiarity is a powerful draw, even for someone as strong as Melinda. It would be ironic if you both were willing to end the relationship for the benefit of the other.

You don't need to get back to me to explain your thoughts—this letter intends to make you aware of Melinda's feelings as I see them. When you discuss all this the next time you see her, she will pick up on your emotions immediately, regardless of your words. She is a perceptive woman despite her young years.

I am afraid I always sound discouraging about your relationship with her. That is not my wish. I would be delighted if you two stayed together. Whatever happens between you, Luke and I will always cherish the time we spent with you, always thinking of you fondly.

Love,

Diane

The ship headed to the nearest port during a brutal storm to ride out the fury. Scott called Melinda on a landline. They spoke, both so flooded with emotion that the beginning of their conversation was slurred. They talked of their shared love and need to see each other. As in her letters, Melinda spoke effusively of her new, independent life. After hanging up, Scott was ebullient and confident, but doubts crept back in soon after. The ship's stay was brief, so he called Julie, the only person who understood all that had happened in Pacific Grove.

"Scott," she screamed, "I'm so glad to hear from you."

They caught each other up on what was happening in their lives, talked about her well-advanced pregnancy, and Scott shared his concerns about Melinda.

Scott said, "Melinda and I have been writing to each other, and I just got off the phone with her. I may be reading too much into her verbal and written words. She still expresses love and hope for our future together. But she also mentions how her life has changed: her own apartment, her return to a job she loved, and her proximity to her parents. I think she enjoys the life she had before Pacific Grove. Her life has been a roller coaster: a long-term relationship ended by death, an intense, brief involvement with me in a different location, and now a long separation."

"Where is this all leading?" Julie asked.

"I find myself considering the old axiom, repeated in prose and songs, that the best expression of love is to let them go. I got a letter from her sister, Diane, mentioning the same points but from a different perspective. She feels that Melinda now views our relationship as an obstacle to my time in the Navy, which includes travel to foreign ports. I'm concerned about interrupting her comfortable life."

Julie paused; Scott could only tell they were still connected by the faint sound of her breathing.

"Is her sister suggesting you end the relationship? Are you considering that?"

"She said the timing is best for everyone to move forward now or reconfirm our commitment to each other."

"In other words, make a decision! I understand your feelings, but I don't know Melinda well enough to offer a firm opinion on whether she would give up all she has now. However, I did you wrong by not telling you about the dangers of involvement with my bridesmaid, so I will tell you my thoughts as long as you understand they are speculative at best."

"Okay, you started with your caveat, so please go ahead."

"I believe she loves you with such depth that it won't fade because of separation. Maybe I'm speaking as a Navy wife who will likely experience time apart from the man I love, but I don't share your doubts."

"How can you be so certain?"

"Clay teases me that I boast of my instincts about people, but he admits I'm often right. Melinda was the most expressive individual I know, conveying her love for you during girl-to-girl moments, how her face lit up when you were together, and especially when she told me of her feelings for you."

"What are you saying?"

"Make no decisions on the future of your relationship until you talk to her face-to-face. You'll know what to do once you look into those lovely eyes. But be prepared to make it clear that you want to stay together for the duration, if that is what you want."

Scott asked, "What does that mean?"

"You'll figure it out."

~ * ~

At the end of two more months, Scott's ship arrived back in San Diego. He carried his gear to the base apartment. Settling in, he made a few phone calls and headed to town to make purchases. The following day, he packed a suitcase and left. Arriving at his destination, he made another call to hail a cab.

Before knocking on the door, he heard people talking in an interior room. Striking the wooden door with his knuckles, a familiar voice called, "I'll get it."

Diane left the dinner table and opened the door. Seeing him, she threw her arms around Scott, whispering, "She doesn't know."

Melinda was in the middle of a conversation with her mother, stopping to ask, "Who was there?" She saw Scott and went silent. Tears formed in her eyes, and she leaped from her chair, flying toward him. Her embrace pushed him back before he could wrap his arms around her waist. Their lips met, and her crying increased.

Luke, Diane, and their parents watched from their seats, smiling at the reunion.

Melinda said, "How...when? I don't know what I'm asking; I'm so overjoyed to see you." Turning toward her family, "Did you all know this?"

They nodded collectively. Her father rose and brought another chair to the table, placing it beside Melinda's seat. After Scott introduced himself to her parents, Mr. Jenkins said, "It's good to match the person against the voice." Scott heard the sound of a foot kicking flesh and hoped Melinda didn't hear.

"Okay, I want to know everything," but before anyone could explain, she asked him, "When did you get back, and how did you know I'd be…"

Scott put a hand on her shoulder. "I'll explain everything; be patient. Diane, do you want to answer in part?"

"When we were in the apartments and the two of you had broken up, I met Scott on the way to the commissary and gave him Mom and Dad's phone number so he could call you in case you hadn't healed your separation before he had to leave. I forgot about it since you gave him your apartment number, but he wouldn't call you anyway. He called here and learned Luke and I had arrived to celebrate Mom's fiftieth birthday with the family. This morning, he called again. Scott, you can pick up from there."

Holding Melinda's hand, he filled in the details. "The ship arrived early yesterday morning, and I arranged my flight here the same day. I called your parents that night and before I took a cab today."

"How long are you staying?" Melinda asked.

"The ship will need some upgrades and general repairs. We won't go to sea for two months. They don't need me or my crew at this point. I've been authorized three weeks' leave."

Mrs. Jenkins said, "You can stay here; in fact, you can have Melinda's old room."

"No way," Melinda shouted. "He's staying with me."

"I thought you'd say that, but don't leave yet. I bet Scott is hungry, and we'd like the chance to know him better." She brought a tray of heated dinner, placing the food before him. Scott ate quickly, anxious to talk more to Melinda's family. Luke asked questions about sea duty, knowing Scott couldn't be specific and Scott asked Luke about his potential orders.

Mr. Jenkins said, "Looking at my daughter's expression, I think she's anxious to leave. I hope we see you a lot during the weeks you're here. Since Melinda is working, you'll have some free time."

"First, I will take him to work to show him off. Then I will ask for a vacation, hoping my boss understands, by appealing to his duty to the country."

~ * ~

Scott and Melinda went to her apartment and, entering, embraced, savoring the closeness. Melinda said, "It's only one bedroom, so we have to share a closet."

Scott put his suitcase alongside the dresser and held her again, slowly inching toward the bed. They undressed quickly, knowing they'd have other times to make love slowly, but at that moment, urgency dictated the speed of foreplay. Then, they settled back on the mattress, satiated.

"I can't count the times I imagined this, lying next to you after making love," Scott said.

"No more than I did," Melinda said, rising on her elbow to kiss him.

They stayed that way, barely moving until Scott rose from the bed.

"I want to see your place," he said as he put his clothes back on.

"Do you want the dressed or undressed tour guide?"

"Dressed, please, or we'll never leave this room."

Melinda gave him a tour of the apartment, but his eyes were only on her.

"Are you hungry?" Melinda asked.

"No, I'm still full from your mother's meal."

"I'll make us some coffee, and we can sit at the table to talk."

After pouring two cups, Melinda put her face in her hands and looked at him.

"It's wonderful to see you; I've missed you so much. I've corresponded with Julie—they are at their new duty station. She had a boy. She sent me a picture of the cutest little guy. Before she delivered, Julie sought recommendations for names, including from me."

"I heard from them that the baby's name is Alexander. Did you mention that was a horse's name?"

"I left out that part."

"Tell me what you've been doing while I was keeping the country safe."

Melinda talked about her job, the challenges in dealing with employee problems, the pleasure of having her own apartment, meeting with friends, going to events, and being near her parents. She stopped suddenly and said, "What are you smiling at?"

"When you are really enthused about something, you speak faster. You must be happy with all you have."

"Of course, I'm pleased with my life, but is there more to your comment—what is it?"

"Your life was in turmoil after your fiancé's death, then uncertain when you moved to Pacific Grove temporarily, and we began our relationship. Nothing you've said now hasn't been apparent in your letters. Your life is full and familiar, but I still offer only that uncertainty."

Melinda took a deep breath and said, "How can you say that, knowing how much I love you? Yes, I like how things are now, but to me, it's only temporary until we can be together. I don't care where or how, but I don't want to be away from you. I only signed a one-year lease on this place and in my performance review at work, I told my boss my future plans were unclear." Her eyes narrowed. "You're lucky you're sitting across from me, or else I'd throttle you for what you're hinting." Her tone softened. "I've kept myself busy, otherwise I'd go crazy thinking about you, missing you. Being home does bring back memories of Teddy, but thoughts of you overshadow those recollections. Why did you have such doubts?"

"I'm busy when we are at sea, but at times at night when I looked at the black sea, I had all sorts of thoughts, some crazy. I want you to be happy, even if not with me. I have about another year with the ship. I likely can get leave again, but it's still a long time apart."

"I'm happy because I know you love me, miss me as much as I miss you, and equally want us to be together. My world without you would collapse; everything I have here would be meaningless."

His eyes were moist. "You make me very happy; I can't picture my life without you, and I promise I will never doubt you, doubt us." Scott grabbed her hands. "I'm sorry."

"If there are any lingering concerns, they will disappear by the end of the three weeks."

"I believe you." Pausing momentarily, he said, "Have you dated anyone?"

"Oh, now you're going to get it."

Melinda jumped up, and he embraced her as she charged toward him.

They sat on the couch, saying little until her eyes grew heavy. In the bedroom, they stripped but had little energy to make love, so she settled against him and fell asleep, he joining her within a few minutes.

~ * ~

Melinda reached for Scott in the morning, but he wasn't there. She called "Scott" in panic.

He came into the room. "Are you okay?"

"I was frightened; I thought I was dreaming you were here," she said, sitting up, her breasts visible.

"You always like to wear my T-shirts in bed. Wait one minute." He flipped open his suitcase to remove a white T-shirt with the ship's name embossed on the front and handed it to her.

Melinda frowned as she put it on. "In your letters, you said you visited ports, but all I get is a T-shirt you probably bought on the ship."

"Not really." Scott knelt at the side of the bed. Reaching down, he lifted a small, wrapped box.

She looked at him, the confusion evident in her expression until she tore off the wrapping paper. Before she could open the box, Scott put his hand over hers, "Will you marry me?"

"Yes," she shouted as she tumbled from the bed beside him on the floor.

They kissed, and he put the ring on her finger.

"You'll be a Navy wife."

"I'm glad I got to know so many wives whose husbands are serving. I'd be honored to be among them. I will welcome those new friends we'll have if Julie is a good example of an officer's wife."

"There are so many plans we need to make. I'm confident my next duty station will be at a base, not shipbound."

She squeezed him. "We need to go to my parents while Diane and Luke are still there, or do they know already?"

"Diane was my co-conspirator."

"Wait a minute—my parents knew, didn't they? I didn't understand why you called my folks' house, now I know."

"I'm old fashioned."

"I want to show them the ring." Melinda coyly asked, "Since I will be an officer's wife, does that mean I outrank my sister?"

They sat together on the floor, leaning against the bed, watching the sun climb to the edge of the window sill.

Meet James Hanley

James Hanley's background includes a career in the military, human resources, and as an adjunct professor. He has had over ninety short stories published in print and online magazines. Transitioning to the longer form, Jim has had novels published by small independent publishers. *Lies Can Sink Love* is his second novel with Wings ePress.

Other Works from the Pen of

James Hanley

Seeking the Future in the Past - Alex, a divorced man in his mid-fifties, announces that he is escaping the stress and losses of his life by meeting with three women of his youth out of curiosity—but is that the real reason?

Dear reader,

I hope you've enjoyed reading this tale of one military man's
complicated deception.

Your opinion is valuable to other
readers like you,
who may be looking for books like mine.

Please consider taking a few minutes to post a review,
however brief,
on the site where you purchased this book
or on the Wings ePress web page.

You may also want to visit my author page
at the Wings' website where you can find the other book I've
published with Wings.

Thank you!

Jim Hanley

Visit Our Website

For The Full Inventory
Of Quality Books:

Wings ePress, Inc

Quality trade paperbacks and downloads
in multiple formats,
in genres ranging from light romantic comedy to general
fiction and horror.
Wings has something for every reader's taste.
Visit the website, then bookmark it.
We add new titles each month!

Wings ePress, Inc.
3000 N. Rock Road
Newton, KS 67114